Andrew R——w

SIXTEEN NOT TOTALLY TEETOTAL

TALL TALES

Andrew Rutherford

Cover design and layout by www.spiffingcovers.com

Printed and bound in Great Britain by TJ International Ltd, Padstow, Cornwall

CONTENTS

TWO'S COMPANY........

Ideas are the children of a lively imagination.

And Brian Woodrow was just a child when he had the idea that he could read people's thoughts, and that once his arms beefed up he would be able to fly.

As a teenager he dreamed he would be much fêted for his 'significant contribution' towards the curing of cancer; triumphantly lift aloft the World Cup, (rugby, football and cricket, obviously); his 100-crew yacht would dwarf a small liner; his books out-sell John Le Carré; his Glastonbury concerts cause a riot — success tumbled over childish success.

But not every success existed only between his two ears, and when he grew up into a graphic designer that lively imagination was worth its weight in gold awards. And hot on their heels, new clients and an almost brand new Bentley.

But, as we shall see, it also led to one quite unintended consequence.

It started when Greta Davis moved into the village, and was followed soon after by Brian taking it into his head to take her into his bed — along with his wife Marcia, of course, for even in this fantasy he would not dream of being unfaithful.

He went weak at the very thought of this delicious ménage à trois.

(So much more acceptable in French, n'est-ce pas?)

But that's where the idea remained — in his thoughts.

For Brian Woodrow did not find it easy to talk to his wife about 'goings on in the bedroom', as his red-faced father had referred to …well… 'goings on in the bedroom.'

Was it this stiff family upbringing or a wife that he still couldn't read with real confidence, that tied his tongue in such knots?

But now, here in libidinous Las Vegas, a city grown fat on hair let down and guards lowered, Brian dared to hope that the idea might seem less offensive, more acceptable to his clever but conservative wife.

But four days had passed, tomorrow they would leave, and still he hadn't plucked up the courage to suggest his three-in-a-bed to Marcia.

But then an opportunity arose that even Brian found too good to miss.

They were eating in a bursting, raucous restaurant with "THE BIGGEST JUICIEST STEAKS IN THE WHOLE US OF A! YEEHAAR!

That was the typically modest Las Vegas claim in four foot high, blood red letters that had guided their hot, tired feet through The Hungry Cowboy's swinging saloon doors, and which now came, in a jolt of inspiration, to Brian's rescue.

'Even 'The biggest juiciest steaks in the whole US of A! Yeehaar!' would become boring if you ate one everyday,' he suggested.

Marcia lifted her wine glass to her lips but didn't answer.

Marcia seldom answered anything but direct questions. Even in the first flush of love he had been mildly disconcerted by this behaviour, and now, after 13 years of marriage, it frankly irritated him.

But irritation had no place in this delicate negotiation.

'Don't you think?' he gently probed.

'Of course they would.'

'A dozen red roses delivered everyday to your door, gift-wrapped in a large pink bow, would be equally tedious after a time', he said.

No answer.

'Wouldn't they?'

'Maybe, but I'd prefer them to the steak, if you're offering', Marcia said, with a hint of a smile — was it a mocking smile? But he must plough on, oblivious to the satisfied roar of a hundred 'hungry cowboys' wolfing down a hundred formidable cows.

'Well'… Brian faltered.

'Well, what?'

'Well it's the same with sex', he blurted out. He was feeling like an adolescent, could feel himself reddening. 'Variety is the spice of life, isn't it?' he added, with what he hoped was a knowing smile but which Marcia saw as a smutty smirk.

She considered him thoughtfully for a while.

'So what is it this time?' she said coolly.

'What do you mean 'what is it this time?' Was she teasing him? Maybe he should change the subject.

'Well', she said with perhaps the faintest hint of disdain, 'when you thought it would be — 'fun' I think was your word for it — to tie my hands to the bedpost, you suggested that even too much foie gras would pall in time.'

'I did?'

'You did. Though as you order it on every possible occasion, perhaps you were wrong.'

She hadn't finished.

'And when you thought it would be a good idea if I were to 'play with myself' for you —'

'Ssh' Brian hissed, darting a nervous glance at the table next to them.

'—I think you used holidays in the Caribbean to make your point.'

'Jesus!' whispered Brian. He had no recollection of saying ...oh, but now he came to think of it...

'Bloody hell', he said 'am I that obvious?'

'Pretty well.' Then after an uncomfortable pause, for him at least, added 'But they were good suggestions, anyway.'

He could hardly have hoped for a more encouraging response.

'I am glad you think so', he ogled.

'So?'

'So what?'

'So, what is it this time?' Marcia seemed genuinely intrigued.

Intrigued now, perhaps, but wouldn't she be shocked, wouldn't she be angry at what he was now screwing up his courage to suggest?

It is true that his wife had agreed to his other cumbersome suggestions to improve their love life without the resistance that he had expected, but now his resolve was deserting him.

'It doesn't matter, it was a joke, really? So, what do you think of this boastful steak?'

'It's good — it hasn't reached the boring stage yet.'

'So what shall we do tomorrow?' he asked, pulling a leaflet from his jacket pocket.

'You're changing the subject. So how do you want to vary our sex lives this time?' And when he didn't answer, she added, 'I hear some people like to be peed on'.

'Marcia! That's sick!'

'I'm glad it wasn't that', she laughed. 'Come on, don't be shy. What was it, then?'

'It wasn't a serious suggestion at all — no, not at all — more a fantasy that all men seem to have...'

'Go on.'

'Oh, you know', he laughed dismissively, 'going to bed with two women at a time.'

'Do they really?' Marcia sounded more curious than shocked.

'Sure. You've seen those telly comedy shows where some guy is always drooling over the prospect. 'Men Behaving Badly', 'Friends'...' he tailed off, as Lorraine, their ever enthusiastic waitress, (cowboy hat, fringed leather jacket, name stenciled onto sheriff's badge) beamed over them.

'How're y'all doin' here, pardners? Ain't that steak just great! Bet you've never tasted better! You want some more wine? We gotta great Napa Valley by the glass.'

Yes, they agreed, the steak was great, they were doing fine, and Brian would like another glass of wine but Marcia wouldn't.

As Lorraine, peeled away to lavish her charm elsewhere in the constant quest for generous tips, Marcia asked, 'And you do, too? Do you fantasize about sleeping with two women?'

'Well...' His chance, so laboriously engineered, had come. Yet still he hesitated.

The clatter of plates, the roar of bawling midwesterners, and their table a small island of silence, until, finally, Marcia broke it.

'You do!' It wasn't a question. It was a revelation.

'Well, er yes, I guess at some level I do.'

'What level, exactly? Do you want another woman to go to bed with us? Is that what you're saying?' At least, he was relieved to see, Marcia had not exploded with disgust or anger.

'It's just a fantasy', he said again, limply.

And there the subject lay, or was put to bed you might say, and half to Brian's relief, and half to his disappointment, they started to discuss their plans for the following day.

They were driving back to their hotel after dinner in their lumbering hired Pontiac, when Marcia asked him how he would feel about them going to bed with another man.

'Don't be ridiculous. You can't tell me that's one of your fantasies, because I just don't believe it.'

She laughed. 'I thought you wouldn't like the idea very much. Yet you expected me to jump at it. All that talk about steaks and roses. Honestly!'

'OK, OK, you've made your point.'

They drove on for a while in silence.

'It's interesting, though,' Marcia said 'your horror at the thought of going to bed with another man is clearly a fear of finding yourself homosexual.'

'Oh please! Spare me the Freud.'

Marcia laughed again; she seemed to be enjoying his discomfort, this discussion, which now he wished he had never started.

'Obviously', she said 'I'm not afraid I might be gay, because the idea of going to bed with another woman doesn't fill me with horror.'

'It doesn't?' There was no mistaking the hopeful surprise in Brian's question.

'Not specially. It isn't something I've given much thought to —'

— 'you've given it some thought, then', Brian interrupted almost too quickly. '*Any* thought to', Marcia corrected herself, 'until this evening. But I can't say the notion is abhorrent.'

'What does that mean?'

'It means I can't say the notion is abhorrent.'

An aggressive blast of hooting jerked Brian's attention back to the road; his fat Pontiac was drifting into the next lane, squeezing two young blacks in a battered Ford Bronco towards a concrete wall. Their shouted obscenities he couldn't hear, their explicit hand actions he couldn't miss. He pulled quickly back into his lane.

The Bronco swerved violently in front of the Pontiac, forcing Brian to stamp on his brakes, then roared away hooting in triumph.

Brian's normal reaction to such aggressive behaviour was a stream of oaths, a blaring protest from the car horn, and an indignant appeal for support from his passengers.

But tonight his concentration was quite elsewhere.

'You were saying that the idea of - you know - three in a bed wasn't abhorrent', he said.

'I had a feeling you wouldn't forget that.'

'Could you imagine the experience being ... pleasant ... fun ... er, exciting, even?'

'I guess that would depend on who it was. Had you anyone in mind? Sue? Ursula? Danni? Bridget?'

'Don't be silly. You've deliberately chosen our least attractive friends.'

'Oh my! They would be charmed to hear that! Who then?' Marcia asked genuinely curious.

Brian was wary. 'I hadn't thought that far ahead. It was only an idea, a fantasy, as I said. I didn't think you'd be so... interested.'

But even as he spoke the words, he was wondering if he dare drop Greta's name casually into the conversation.

He didn't have to.

'What about Greta? To a man you simper around her —oozing all that Scandinavian sex appeal.'

'Greta?' Brian's genuine surprise at Marcia's suggestion spared him the trouble of faking it.

Greta Davies (Greta pronounced as in 'better' not 'beat her' as she insisted at every introduction) was a divorcee who had moved into the village two years earlier, and, as all the wives had observed, set the pulses racing of their 'pathetically predictable' men.

A striking blue-eyed blond, slim and vivacious, Greta Davies could have stepped straight from the pages of a brochure from the Swedish Tourist Board. Her popularity with every male under 80 in the village, and some over, was assured, but it was greatly enhanced by her ability to give every man she talked to the inescapable feeling that he was the most charming and witty man in the county.

Brian included.

How could he have failed to notice the particular sparkle in Greta's eyes when she spoke to him, the hand touching his arm so often, the quick kiss on the mouth instead of the cheek when they met, her delighted laugh at his jokes.

But how could he have failed to notice that every other male present received similar breathless attention.

'So you weren't thinking of Greta as a bed buddy?' Marcia persisted.

'I told you, it was a fantasy... nobody was in my mind. Although, since you mention it, I suppose Greta could fill the bill.'

'Or fill the bed?'

'Or fill the bed.'

They drove on in silence — Brian reluctant to force the issue and perhaps invite an unconsidered rejection. He had planted the seed, he would give it time to grow. And he was pleased that he had finally plucked up the courage to plant it.

And was it the red-blooded steak, the wine by the glass or his suggestion that made Marcia particularly responsive that night in their 'Henry The Eighth King Sized Bed', and encouraged Brian to hope that the seed had not fallen on barren ground?

Like those exotic bottles of unlikely and now untouched liqueurs — so moor-ish in Marakesh, so tempting in Taipei — great ideas brought home from far way places seldom have the same appeal when tested in the cold light of an English autumn day. Or night.

And Brian, back in their own familiar bed in their tidy and polite Cotswold village, slipped back into the comforts of monogamy like an otter into a lake — with barely a ripple.

When he recalled the conversations he and Marcia had in Nevada, it was with more uneasiness than desire.

How could he have imagined that his rather staid Marcia would take his suggestion seriously for a moment?

Ah well, a little daydreaming thousands of miles from the real world... no harm done. But now he hoped Marcia would forget all about it.

But Marcia didn't.

Not for the first time Brian had misjudged his wife — and her response to his suggestion.

When Marcia had told Brian that she had never imagined being in bed with another woman, she wasn't being totally honest. True, she had never thought of a threesome with Brian or anybody else. But in the early days of their marriage when Brian's love-making had been clumsy and selfish, and her enjoyment with a man had been so unsatisfactory, she *had* wondered how she might feel with a woman.

Did she have lesbian leanings, she had vaguely wondered.

And when she had imagined being in bed with Catherine Deneuve — the woman Brian drooled over at the time — she had found the idea mildly titillating, but not nearly as exciting as sleeping with Robert Redford.

'So', she had decided, 'I'm not a lesbian. Brian just isn't Robert Redford'.

So the years had passed, a little variety added, and Marcia had come to terms with their 'goings on in the bedroom'.

But Brian's tentative suggestion had reawakened the dispiriting feeling that other women were enjoying a far more rewarding sex life than she was, and she examined the idea of adding Greta to their bed at first with mild interest and then with growing curiosity.

When they had returned to England she had expected Brian to blunder around to the subject again — the tedium of too much Mozart, perhaps.

But he hadn't, and Marcia suspected his reticence was due to her faint-hearted reaction in Las Vegas rather than any cooling of his own enthusiasm.

So she decided to take the initiative.

And the first time she found herself in Greta's company, Marcia had studied her with new eyes. She had looked at Greta's breasts, her legs and her lips, just as she imagined Brian would, and found that her heart was beating faster, and she felt herself blushing when Greta spoke to her.

And later that very night she rang Greta, and heart pounding again, suggested they had lunch together one day.

'Good idea', Greta sounded enthusiastic, 'what about tomorrow?'

'Tomorrow?' Marcia had hoped for a little longer to change her mind if her nerve faltered.

'Is Friday any good for you?', she asked.

'No. I can't make Friday, and next week looks hopeless. Tomorrow no good?'

'OK, tomorrow.' Marcia blurted out.

Marcia's gallery in Cheltenham is not half a mile from the travel agency that Greta managed and part owned, and there is no shortage of good places to eat in the town, and yet they opted to meet at a small intimate restaurant in Winchcombe, eight miles away.

Quite why, neither could have said, but perhaps both sensed the need to step outside their everyday environment.

But here they were, spending more than they meant, and feeling delightfully irresponsible.

After two glasses of wine, and while Marcia was still dithering over the menu, Greta asked why she had suggested the lunch.

'Why not?' Marcia replied, a little too loudly.

'Well, you never have before. Most of the other wives have at one time or another.'

'Have they?' The sudden picture of Greta making a threesome with all the couples in the village, made Marcia laugh out loud.

'Well, that's a good reason to ask you now', she said.

'You have a lovely laugh, Marcia. It's very ... infectionous. Is that the word?'

'More or less, yes', Marcia said, trying not to look too long into Greta's beautiful blue eyes.

'I'm so glad we are meeting, properly, at last', Greta purred, 'I've admired you, secretly, ever since I came to live in the village.'

Marcia found herself blushing with pleasure. My, these Scandinavians were so direct.

'There's not much to admire about me, I'm afraid', she said.

'Oh you English, you drive me mad, with all that false modesty!'

'No, I mean it, I — '

'You are beautiful', Greta interrupted, impatiently 'clever, funny, attractive, which isn't the same as beautiful, deep I should think, and very sexy, I bet.'

'Oh!' gasped Marcia.

The waiter glided over deferential, friendly, superior.

'Have you decided, mesdames?' He wasn't French, just a little smug.

'The scallops please, and the sea bass', Marcia ordered, impulsively.

'Me, as well'. Greta, who had scarcely glanced at the menu, gave him the full beam of her most dazzling smile.

He subsided like a souffle, and shuffled back to the serving hatch, there to gaze at this gorgeous customer, quite impervious to the growing impatience of the other diners trying to catch his eye.

'What were we talking about?' Greta asked.

'Er, well, I think it was about me.'

'Of course it was. I said I bet you are very sexy. Am I right?'

'Yes you're right, that is what you said', Marcia laughed.

'And am I right?' Greta's unblinking blue eyes stared deep into Marcia's and with a flood of pleasure Marcia understood that there was nothing she need hide from the lovely woman across the table.

'OK.' Marcia said as deliberately as a thumping heart and sudden shortness of breath would allow, 'I asked you to lunch because I wanted to ...suggest ...oh God!... you might like to...' she faltered.

'Go to bed with you? Yes please.' Greta's eyes hadn't left Marcia's for an instant.

The waiter approached with the expensive scallops that Marcia knew she would not eat. Could not eat.

The sun warms them through the window, tourists wander aimlessly through the town outside, a pan drops in the kitchen, in the distance a police siren getting fainter. But Marcia hears nothing but the buzzing in her head, feels nothing but the pressure of Greta's hand on hers and sees nothing but Greta's beautiful, beautiful face.

Later. Marcia is lying in Greta's arms in Greta's bed in Greta's house. They have made love three times and Marcia is exhausted and elated and thoroughly confused.

Greta's lack of inhibition has awakened her own. She has done and said things with a guiltless joy that has amazed and delighted her. And would certainly shock Brian, she imagines.

And what about Brian? She hasn't given him a moment's thought, and soon she must go back to him. What will she do then? Nothing seems clear.

'Brian will be expecting me back'. She says. 'What shall I tell him, I wonder?'

'You met me for lunch, and we went on a shopping spree —no, you've bought nothing — and we went to the pictures — ah, but then he will ask about the film. You met me for lunch and we went to bed!' Greta laughs, not a care in the world.

'It's alright for you!' Marcia sighs.

'It certainly was alright for me.' Greta stretches out to stroke Marcia's leg, but is pushed gently away.

'It was Brian who suggested you might like to go to bed with me'—

'You're joking!'

'—and with him. He thought a threesome might brighten up our marriage.'

'I see.' Marcia hears the hurt in Greta's voice and is surprised.

'And do you still think that would be a good idea?' asks Greta.

'No.'

'Nor do I. I've done three-in-a-bed. It doesn't 'brighten up a marriage', I can tell you.'

'Your marriage?'

'Not mine, my best friend's. My ex-best friend's. Her husband left her and followed me around Stockholm like a sick dog.'

Marcia says nothing, and after a long pause, 'I must be going Greta. It was breathtaking.'

'But you won't repeat the experience.' Greta seemed quite sure of that, and not at all upset. It helped Marcia to be honest.

'No, Greta, I won't. The truth is I am not a ...well you know...that way inclined.'

'Nor me, actually.'

'It was…what was it?…an experiment, I suppose. I hope you understand.'

'Oh, we Swedes are very understanding.'

Brian has left a message on the answer phone. He's going to a late meeting, and won't be back till 9pm.

'Perhaps he's having an affair,' thinks Marcia. She has never thought that before, no matter how often he has been late.

'Or perhaps I'm just thinking that so I can feel less guilty,' muses Marcia, ' but do I feel guilty?' She comes to the conclusion that she doesn't. She's had an extraordinary afternoon of passion - it was a huge release, and she is at peace. But she has no wish to repeat it. She is quite sure of that.

She can't wait for Brian to get back, and although it's nearer 10pm when he does, she greets him with a large glass of red wine and a great big bear hug.

'What's all that about?', he asks, pleased but surprised.

'Oh. You know. Nothing and everything.'

'Well, that's nice.' Then after the shortest of pauses, 'Is there anything to eat? I'm starving.'

'Yes, it's steak', she giggles ' the non-boring kind', then hollers 'Y-E-E-H-A-R!'

He smiles but he's baffled. 'You're in a very jolly mood. Have you been at the wine by any chance?'

'I may have had a glass, Brian.'

'Or two?'

'Or two.'

MR EASTHAM CREEPS OUT OF HIS SHELL

We'd like to introduce Horace Eastham.

He'd fight tooth and nail to resist it.

Horace is as near as our village gets to a recluse.

'Good company' is to Horace a contradiction in terms; and the lengths he goes to avoid it are both comical and sad.

But on the rare occasions when all his evasions are overcome, then he resorts to his notorious 'crib sheet'.

This crib sheet is the source of great amusement to the villagers — until they find themselves, disconcertingly, on the wrong end of it.

It contains a list of questions which he unfolds onto the table in front of him and refers to whenever a conversation can no longer be avoided.

1. Social. 2. Current Affairs. 3. Local Events.

Should you find yourself sitting next to Horace at a supper party he will glance at you furtively, study his crib sheet and select a question he deems appropriate.

For example, from 1. Social: 'Do you have children? And if so, how do you consider their education could be improved?'

And when you have replied, with as much enthusiasm as you can muster to an audience who is clearly not listening, he will peruse his sheet again, and read from, say, 3. Local Events: 'I understand the ancient church pews may be replaced. What are the pros and cons in your opinion?'

'I felt as though I was sitting an exam', Deborah Willard remarked after one such strained session with Horace, 'and any moment he'll say, "Time's up, put down your pens." It's all very odd.'

'Very odd, but very Horace Eastham.' They all agreed.

Horace Eastham rents a large rambling flat above the Grade 2 listed stables of Marcus and Julia Strickland's grand Georgian mansion.

Marcus inherited this handsome pile set in 800 acres of park and farmland from a grandfather who made a pile of his own by putting marmalade on the king's toast.

He also put marmalade on a very great quantity of less exalted toast, altogether more humble toast, but it's the marmalade in the Crown Derby dish on the silver tray in the footman's white gloved hand at Windsor Castle that the Stricklands recall, and often, with the greatest satisfaction.

In the 'good old days' of pitiful wages, Horace's flat housed two coachmen and three valets from the 'big house' 100 yards to the East — but is barely large enough to contain one untidy and obsessive collector.

It is true that the low ceilings and lower doors are not ideal for someone as awkward and tall as Horace ('6 foot 6.6

inches or 200 cms' he would admit to if pressed), but a few bumps on the head are a small price to pay for the complete quiet and seclusion that he loves and values so much.

He is a teacher at Pate's Grammar school in Cheltenham, where, to the surprise of all, he enjoys a remarkable rapport with his students and, to the surprise of none, equally awkward relations with his fellow teachers.

His peers may sneer down at his stunted social development but must crane their necks to peer up at his towering intellect, not a combination to allow for easy communication between them.

Horace graduated from Cambridge with the highest prize of his year — a Double First in Philosophy and Theology of 'Especial Distinction' — and was immediately offered a Fellowship by his College, St John's, which he refused in favour of the position at Pate's, the school he had attended as a boy.

It was a baffling decision from a baffling man.

Not only would he certainly have flourished as an eccentric Fellow at the ancient University, but also his days as a pupil at the school had been particularly miserable.

The only child of a vicar and a tall, domineering vicar's wife he had been identified immediately, with the tiresome instinct of eleven year olds, as a brainy loner with a silly name and bullied from his very first day at the school. Bullying which stopped rather smartly when he shot up to a boney six foot and still growing.

He had been an avid collector. Every living thing — with the notable exception of the race to which he belonged — aroused his passionate interest.

Grasses, birds' eggs, butterflies, moths, barks, insects, leaves, seeds; all were lovingly gathered, tabulated and indexed, until his room at the vicarage, and then the rambling attic and then part of the basement were slowly filled with a formidable variety of cardboard, tin and plastic boxes, and inside them an even greater variety of specimens.

Charles Darwin, himself, would not have been ashamed of such a hoard.

Everybody at Pate's and his parents had been astonished, therefore, when he had opted not to read Biology or Natural sciences at Cambridge, but Philosophy and Theology.

'They force me to think more deeply', he had explained.

And to judge from the weighty tomes on the floor-to-ceiling bookshelves in his flat, and the piles of magazines and yet more books that had spilled over onto every floor, thinking more deeply was for Horace Eastham the very breath of life.

You could feel him thinking more deeply as he brushed past you, unseeing, in the street, or as he strode over the Cotswolds, his long hair flying out behind him as though hanging on for dear life to those very same very deep thoughts.

No wonder he refused so many invitations where conversations revolved around cars, children, and house prices, none of which he had invested in, or the stock market or politics, neither of which for him held the least interest.

Nevertheless Horace Eastham did feel reluctantly obliged to accept the occasional invitation from the Stricklands. As a tenant he supposed he was expected to.

And so one Saturday evening Horace found himself cornered by Greta Davies in what Julia and Marcus called the 'small ballroom'.

Should you be tactless enough to ask Julia about the large ballroom, with, perhaps, the tiniest implication that she was putting on airs, she was quite unabashed.

'Oh goodness, no. There isn't a large ballroom. The small ballroom was so named by Sir Joseph Strickland when he bought the house in 1937. Sir Joseph, that's Marcus's grandfather, you know, was the jam King of England, and indeed the King of England ate his jam. They used to say that there wasn't a house in the country without a jar of Strickland jam or Strickland marmalade in the cupboard...' and Julia would recount at some considerable length the very satisfactory history that concluded with her as mistress of this very same 'small ballroom' seventy nine years later.

On the Saturday when Horace met Greta this very ballroom was crowded with the relaxed and the smiling in their carefully chosen 'smart casual' clothes, a glass of wine in one hand, a canapé in the other — greedily grabbed from the elegant young caterers weaving amongst them — and an unwavering self-assurance reflected in their faces.

Or that's how they appeared to Horace, in his ill-fitting suit, a glass of water in one hand, his crib sheet ready in the other, and a look of near panic in his eyes.

He had stationed himself in the far corner behind the piano, where he hoped he would be ignored by the rest of the party — a hope that might have been fulfilled, most of the guests only too happy to allow someone else the pleasure of Horace's company — had it not been for Greta Davies.

She noticed him as soon as she entered the room. She had heard all about Horace, of course, for the harder he tried to avoid the public gaze the more he attracted it.

Now she smiled at his futile attempts to be inconspicuous — half hidden behind the piano, half facing the wall, stooping as if to hide his height, his shock of long greying hair, his eyes darting from side to side like a cornered rabbit, the poor man stood out like a beacon.

She was very curious to meet this unusual man.

But was it just curiosity, or did Horace represent a challenge to the flirtatious Swedish beauty? She knew all too well that men — Englishmen, at least — were attracted to her, and enjoyed encouraging their attention. But this one, she thought, this one would challenge her charms to the limit.

But, 'varfor inte', it would be an amusing way to pass an hour at the party.

And so, like a hunter creeping up on a timorous feeding deer, Greta moved cautiously in his direction — greeting friends here, accepting a canapé there, a kiss on the cheek from Ian Willard, laughing prettily at a Graham Porter joke she didn't understand, conscious of the usual husbands stealing glances in her direction, but all the time edging closer to her nervous prey.

And then she was at the piano, blocking his line of retreat. The sudden alarm in his eyes was all the welcome she had expected. My goodness the man was timid.

'Hello' she smiled her warmest smile 'I don't think we've met....well I know that we haven't met...I'm sure I would have remembered such an...interesting man. I'm Greta...as in 'better', not Greta as in 'beat her'. Just remember you'd better not beat her.'

She laughed and held out her hand, but it wasn't taken. He was trapped, his escape route blocked, he shifted his feet as though about to bolt, but she held her ground.

She could see the famous crib sheet in his hand. How soon would he use it? she wondered.

'Are you going to keep me in suspense?' she fluttered.

'In suspense?'

'Do you have a name?'

'Of course.' And then after a long painful pause, and as this woman seemed to expect more, added, 'I'm Mr. Eastham.'

'And do you have a Christian name Mr. Eastham?'

'My first name is Horace.'

'So you're not a Christian, Horace?'

For a split-second he glanced at her. But was looking straight at the wall when he felt obliged to defend his faith against this total stranger's accusation.

'My father was a vicar. Neither he nor my mother neglected my Christian education. Certainly not.'

Greta who had dug the hole that he had blindly stepped into, now felt obliged to help him out of it. 'Only you said your first name was Horace, not your Christian name was Horace.'

'I see, yes.' Another long pause, again her look of expectancy, so, again, he felt obliged to add more .'I am a teacher at a multi-faith school. The term Christian name is discouraged.'

'I guessed as much, I was teasing you, Horace. It was very naughty of me.'

He looked at her again, this time for more than a split-second, and she rewarded him with her most enticing smile. He relaxed just a fraction, from Red to High Alert. Perhaps this woman was just a little less threatening than most.

'Teasing is the cross we teachers have to bear', he smiled timidly back, 'although I shouldn't say 'cross to bear' for the reasons mentioned above.'

She laughed prettily at his little joke. 'I've heard a lot about you Horace Eastham', she said

'You have?' Startled again, immediately wary, back to Red Alert.

'Yes. I've heard that you are absolutely brilliant.'

If she had hoped that he would modestly deny the charge or puff with pride, or even blush, she was to be disappointed.

He had often been told how clever he was, and, paradoxically, he was the only one in the room that evening who was clever enough to refute it.

For every book he had read, there were a hundred he hadn't, for every fact he had absorbed there were a thousand he never would. No, he was not 'absolutely brilliant', on the contrary, he was dismayed at his own ignorance. Why didn't this woman just go away and leave him in peace? And how soon could he leave the party without seeming rude?

Flattery clearly having failed Greta tried another tack. 'In fact, I hear that you are so brilliant you find it impossible to talk to silly people like me.'

Horace, clearly mortified at this accusation, shook his head vigorously and, quite against his inclination, blurted out:

'Yes, I do find it hard to talk to people. It's not because I am so clever. I am so stupid, I can never think what to say.'

'Is that why you carry that sheet of paper?' she asked gently.

He looked at the paper in his hand, and back to her. She was very pretty he saw now, her expression was open and almost childlike. He could talk to children. He relaxed a little more.

'Yes', he said simply. He looked at the paper again, and stuffed it in his pocket. 'It's only a few questions.'

'And what question would you like to ask me?' Greta said. 'No, don't read one from your list'. She added, as he automatically reached for his crib sheet.

He hesitated and then withdrew his hand without his lifeline.

'I would say from your accent that you are from Sweden, am I right?' He asked.

'You are right, yes. But can you tell which part, there are many regional dialects?'

'Stockholm', he said immediately.

'Goodness!' She clapped her hands. 'You're a real Professor Higgins. Yes, Stockholm is right. How clever.'

'No, it was just a silly guess. Twenty-one percent of all Swedes live in Stockholm, so it was a possibility, but I'd be vexed with my students if they guessed an answer with such a large chance of error.'

'In an exam, yes of course, but this is a party. You're allowed to say silly things at a party.'

But he didn't say a silly thing, he didn't say anything. He looked round the room hearing the babble of voices, imagining the torrent of silly things.

'You don't like parties, do you, Horace?'

He looked at her properly then. She was quite lovely, an open smile, a playful look in her eyes. His hope that she would move quickly on, as most people, to his relief, always did, weakened. Now he would not be too distressed if this woman - what was her name? - would stay.

'I'm sorry I've forgotten your name', he said.

'Greta Davies. Greta as in better', she said again ,'It's how we say it in Sweden.'

'Greta as in better', he repeated,

She waited for the polite pleasantry . 'What a pretty name', perhaps, but pleasantries were not Horace's strong suit.

'You haven't answered my question', she said, 'but you don't need to, I can see that you hate parties. I expect you're just wishing I'd go away and leave you in peace.'

Such blatant fishing for a denial, which might have provoked an insincere gallantry from most men, quite alarmed Horace Eastham.

'Oh no', he protested earnestly, 'not at all. If you go you won't leave me in peace, you'll leave me in... Limbo, again. No, you are quite correct, I'm not very good at parties.'

'I find the wine helps.' She looked at his glass. 'Is that water or a strong gin?'

'It's water. I did try drinking to help me through occasions like this' ...he stopped, and shuddered at the memory.

'Shall we go and get something to eat?' Greta asked impulsively, 'There's a buffet in the dining room, and when I last looked there were still a few chairs free.'

He was surprised and yes, he was pleased. This attractive woman — Greta — actually appeared to welcome his company. And he, for once in his life, was not unhappy to share it.

'Well, er ...yes, I could manage that', he said. And he was enticed, at last, from his sanctuary by the piano.

'You can tell me all about yourself.' she said as they moved through the surprised glances from one end of the 'small ballroom' to the other.

'Oh, there's nothing to say about me', he said.

And then for the next two hours he talked about himself non-stop. His crib sheet long forgotten, coaxed on by Greta, his debilitating shyness slowly fell away, and he found himself sharing thoughts and feelings that he had never revealed to a living soul.

At first Greta listened to Horace with considerable satisfaction. It was a triumph of sorts to win so many confidences from this famously bottled up man. And when the lonely, so accustomed to talking only to themselves, find a receptive audience they have so much stored away desperate to be aired.

And Horace, uncorked, talked. And talked. And talked. His lonely years in the vicarage, his distant father and unloving mother, his envy of children with brothers and sisters...and on and on...through his awful school days...his collecting...the bullying...

But when he was in full spate, and all coaxing was quite unnecessary, Greta's attention started to wander. She could see her friends watching the two of them with wonder. They would be agog to learn how she'd contrived to draw out this tight-lipped, chronically shy man, although some no doubt would make a not altogether complimentary guess.

She was concerned, too, by the growing urgency of the monologue — for she it appeared had no part to play, except as an ear. She did feel sympathy for this unusual man, for she herself was not immune to loneliness, but was he revealing truths that he would later regret?

Should she stop him? But how? He would be badly hurt if he thought she had lost interest. That much was clear, so earnestly was his attention focussed on her. And himself.

Oh well, she'd started it, she'd just have to see it through, hear him out. She wanted to talk to Brian and Marcia, particularly Marcia, but there was no chance of that. She turned her attention back to Horace.

It was past midnight when she finally made her excuses and left the party.

She was exhausted.

Horace Eastham left immediately after her.

He was exhilarated.

...AND NOTHING BUT THE TRUTH.

Vivienne Ward pulls a sheet of paper from the drawer, rummages around for a pen, sits down at the kitchen table and writes:-

Derek Henderson. Pros and Cons.

She underlines it.

Derek Henderson. Pros and Cons
1. 'Pros':-

For some time she stares at the empty sheet while she picks and picks at distant memories that like a scab are best left well alone.

A sudden movement pulls her gaze into the garden, to see 'that bloody ginger tom' landing in her nasturtiums from the neighbour's fence.

It settles down to its daily poo. She shouts and bangs on the window to no effect, then turns angrily back to the paper in front of her, scores out *Pros* and writes, prompted by the cat perhaps:-

> 2.*'Cons:-'*
> *A self-satisfied shit*

When Derek Henderson's letter clattered through sixty-two letterboxes it provoked intrigue, irritation, approval and disdain.

One irked response: 'Oh, it's so like Derek Henderson. He craves attention like a child. I, for one, shan't indulge him.'

And a kinder one: 'It's an interesting idea and very courageous. But I wouldn't dream of sending a letter like that.'

Like what?

Like this.

> *4, Cotswold Place*
> *Campden Lane*
> *Near Winchcombe*
> *Gloucestershire*
> *GL 12 3XB*
>
>   *21st September 2016*
> *Dear ....*
>
> > *"Oh wad some Power the giftie gie us*
> > *To see oursels as ithers see us"*
>
> *I've never been a great Robbie Burns fan, but that insight has always intrigued me.*
> *Clearly Burns believes we would all benefit*

from knowing what other people think of us. But would we?

And if we did know would it alter how we thought about ourselves?

I am fascinated by the idea. Enough, even, to try and find out.

And that's the purpose of this letter.

You are the Power with the 'giftie' to show me 'as ithers' see me.

I want you to tell me exactly what you think of me - warts and all.

No holds barred.

Don't be polite or flattering (unless, of course, you think I deserve it!) or imagine that I will take offence if you're not.

I daresay that some of you will find this very presumptuous or even plain daft, but I do hope you'll take the request seriously, all the same.

I'm excited if a little nervous at the prospect.

I've stuck my head above the parapet, so feel free to have a pot at it.

To save me from living in total suspense for an unfixed period, may I ask that you send me your 'critique' by October the 8th. Ursula and I leave for the Galapagos tomorrow morning and we get back on the 8th. To find, I hope, a mountain of letters or even emails from all you 'ithers'.

Darwin formed a great insight in the Galapagos. Perhaps I will get an insight about myself when I get back. Please indulge me.

Yours very, very sincerely

Derek
PS. I have sent husbands and wives separate letters — you might see me in quite different lights.

****

The fat black tyres of the Hendersons' jumbo jet had barely lifted off the runway at Heathrow before Deborah Willard was on the 'phone to Marcia Woodrow at her gallery in Cheltenham.

'Well Marcia! What do you make of that!? I presume you got one too.'

'Derek's letter?'

'You won't answer it will you?'

She was hoping that her smart, successful friend, to whom she so often but quite unconsciously referred, would reinforce her own considerable reluctance to reply.

'Yes, I think I probably will. He seems keen that we should.'

'Oh dear, will you really?' And after a pause added, 'So what will you say?'

'That would be telling.'

'He just wants us to tell him how original he is.'

'Apparently he's not fishing for compliments, Debs.'

He swans off to the Galapagos looking for blue footed bambies and expects us to drop everything ——'

'Boobies.'

'What?'

'Blue footed Boobies.'

For some seconds there was no reply.

'Deborah?'

'Yes, I'm still here. I was just thinking. In a small intimate community like ours keeping any secrets is a miracle...never mind sharing them. I don't want to know too much about anyone. And I certainly don't want anyone to know too much about me.'

These were not spontaneous thoughts. Deborah had been worrying them out since the post had arrived and she was anxious for her friend to agree. Marcia understood that, but pretended not to.

'So you won't be answering Derek's letter?' she said.

'No, no. I wouldn't know where to start.'

****

It is entirely possible that golfers are capable of robust, independent thoughts in the privacy of their own homes, but once they've pulled on their plus-fours any such individuality flies out of the locker room window.

So it will come as no surprise to learn that the members of the Naunton Downs Golf Club did not treat Derek Henderson's letter with the personal and deliberate attention that the writer hoped.

It was open house for a good deal of shared mirth. Led, for the most part, by those whose opinions Derek had clearly not valued, and so felt all the more determined to give.

'I suppose we should tell him that he's lifting his head on the backswing?'

'Or shifting his weight onto the wrong foot on his follow through?'

'Or taking too many practise swings before each shot?'

'And will keep taking putts out of turn?'

'Well, he did ask for the whole truth.'

The joke rumbled on for days.

'Is anyone going to take his letter seriously, do you suppose?' pondered Roger Hawes one morning when rain had driven them back into what golfers call the 'nineteenth', and anyone else would call the bar.

It was a question, like most questions, on which Andy Grice had a firm view.

'In my opinion we don't know him well enough', he stated categorically. 'Let's face it, all we talk about is golf. If we are not boasting about our good shots, we're grumbling about our bad luck.'

'Like the drive you sliced over the road and into the cricket field from the twelfth tee.' Peter Tewson smirked. 'Rotten luck, that.'

A comment Andy chose not to hear.

'OK, we might talk about cars, boast about our kids or the value of our houses, but what does that tell us? Bugger all. It's irrelevant, anyway. In my opinion he's a perfectly good club member. That's all you need to know. A good club member. Wouldn't mind that on my gravestone. And as far as I'm concerned, that's the end of it.'

'It certainly would be', Peter Tewson wisecracked, and everybody laughed except Andy.

****

A self-satisfied shit!'

Viv Ward surprised herself when she impulsively scribbled down those few crude words. It was all so long ago. But now digging it up again she found the hurt still sharp.

Was that what Derek Henderson wanted? To remind her what a great lover he had been?

Ha!

She gazed towards the gentle meadows beyond her country garden but saw only the cramped flat dwarfed by Victoria Station and the narrow bed where she and Derek had grappled and panted — a tie hanging on the bedroom doorknob to warn his flatmate that he had 'company'.

Viv was working as a receptionist at one of London's most distinguished Law Firms when Derek Henderson had pushed through the imposing revolving door and walked into her life.

It was his first day as an articled clerk at Blackwood and Penn, and he might be expected, perhaps, to have shown just a modicum of apprehension, but no, he had breezed in brimming with confidence.

'Hello' big white-teeth smile. 'I'm Derek and you're very pretty.'

'What is your name?' she asked coldly, 'and who have you come to see?'

'Sorry, much too forward.' He said, still smiling. 'The name's Derek Henderson, I'm to be articled here. I've come to see Mr. Lanbury.'

And when Mrs. Robinson, Lanbury's 50 year old secretary, came down to fetch him, and was walking ahead of him towards the lift Derek said baldly to Viv, 'Would you like to go for a glass of wine one day?'

'How very kind', Mrs. Robinson had replied without turning. ' Shall I bring my husband? Or perhaps my children? They're about your age.'

Vivienne Winchester, 19, lived in a hostel for 'Young Ladies of Quality' in Gloucester Road, favoured by nervous county folk for daughters taking their first timid steps into the great metropolis.

While other girls her age shared boisterous flats, gossiped and flirted at clubs and pubs, Viv would leave her dignified but subdued workplace, at 5.30pm to the minute, and return to her less dignified but equally subdued small room.

The nervous expectations with which she had arrived in London were fast fading and every weekend she hurried home to Mummy and Daddy and Blackie the dog in Berkhamsted.

But the nervous expectations were rekindled when within days Derek Henderson again invited her for a drink — this time less bumptiously — and she accepted.

So, one warm summer's evening Viv did not trudge back to Gloucester Road but settled back into Derek's sporty new Mazda MX -5 — 'One of the veryfirst in London' he bragged — and was driven to The Dove pub, on the river at Hammersmith.

As the car snaked and snarled through the traffic and the warm air had whipped her chestnut hair round that 'very pretty' face she had finally felt a small flutter of hope in this great indifferent capital city.

That evening Derek was all 'Pros' and no 'Cons' — funny and charming and attentive, and as warm as the sun which dazzled off the river when they arrived, and moved West to drop into Chiswick in a blaze of scarlet. And they talked and laughed and talked, and Viv didn't think once about Berkhamsted, and home and Blackie.

It was a fine summer for an open-topped sports car and Derek was pleased to have such an attractive passenger to show off in his noisy new toy. A hundred miles into the country, half a mile to a cinema or a pub, no journey too long or short but they must jump into the MX -5 and, like Viv's feelings for the driver, race away.

But there were signs, which Viv tried not to recognise, that those feelings were not fully reciprocated.

Once they found themselves within a mile of Viv's home in Berkhamsted, but for all her entreaties Derek firmly declined the chance to 'pop in for a quick visit to meet mummy and daddy and Blackie'.

And as the summer waned the car was far more likely to be found parked outside Derek's pokey flat than the latest club or smart restaurant.

Like the heroines of the romantic novels that Viv devoured, she dreamed of being crushed in a passionate manly embrace, but Derek's ardent kisses proved to be less Georgette Heyer than a means to her end.

Viv tried hard to relax as she and Derek made uncomfortable love on his lumpy three foot wide bed, but frankly she got more pleasure from their outings in his noisy little car. Couldn't he be just a little more romantic?

Then, out of the blue, he took her to a smart hotel in Sussex for the weekend and all Viv's misgivings were swept away.

So the shock was all the greater when a girl at the office saw Derek in a restaurant with a blonde. That's all Viv ever knew about her. She was blonde. 'She and Derek had looked very close', Denise had told her spitefully.

'Denise Peterson told me she saw you at a restaurant with a blonde. She said you looked very close.' They were standing in the small kitchen in his flat, and Derek was pouring a none-too-chilled Chardonay into two none-too-clean mugs.

'Good old Denise. Such a trouble maker.' He said.

'So who was she, this blonde?'

He thought briefly of lying. That he didn't, said more about his waning attraction to Viv, than his honesty.

'She was a girl I met at a party in the country', he said.

'And are you 'very close'? As Denise said?'

'I suppose we are quite close, yes.'

Viv bit her lip, and turned away to hide the tears that were racing to her eyes.

She expected him to say more, to make excuses, to explain, to apologise... but he just lifted his mug of wine and sipped from it.

'And were you going to tell me about her?' Viv said as calmly as the mounting anger and hurt would allow.

'We have a great relationship, Viv, I didn't want to spoil it.'

She struck his face so hard that she knocked the mug of wine, lifted to his lips, clean out of his hand. 'Christ!' He lifted his hand to his face, bright red from the blow. 'What the fuck are you doing?'

'You didn't want to spoil our relationship!' she screamed at him. 'You didn't want to spoil our relationship! Don't you think being 'very close' to some blonde you met at a party might spoil our relationship?'

She was crying now and Derek tried to put his arm around her, but she flung it off.

'I suppose you expected to just carry on with both of us! Is that it? It was just too bad that Denise saw you together. Is that what you think? Has she been here in your bed?'

He hesitated for a fraction of a second too long.

'No.'

She slumped into the threadbare armchair.

'You're being very melodramatic, Viv. What do you expect me to say?'

40

'Will you stop seeing this blonde?'

He picked up the mug, and put it in the sink.

'Well, will you?' she asked again.

'Do you want me to choose between you?'

'I thought we were 'very close', she sobbed.

'We were', he said, 'but face it Viv, neither of us expected it to be a long term thing.'

'Oh', she said with as much irony as she could through her tears, 'you forgot to mention that when you were puffing away so ineffectively in that horrid bed!'

They never spoke at the office. She saw him coming and going, of course. Sometimes alone, but more often with friends, laughing and jostling at the revolving door, or carrying great piles of Mr. Lanbury's papers as he deferentially followed the great man to court, but she pointedly ignored him. Which was silly because she did miss him badly and when she was called to the 'phone in the hostel one evening at the time he used to call, her heart did race.

'Hello.'

'Hello Viv. It's Jim.'

'Jim?' Her mind a blank.

'Jim Ward. Derek Henderson's flat mate. We met here, at the flat.'

'The copywriter?' Had he news about Derek? Was he ringing as a peacemaker at Derek's request? Was Derek there with him, now? Had he dropped the blonde?

Her hopes, like Icarus, soared in vain.

'That's right. A copywriter at Bradshaw and Buckingham. That's why I'm ringing. The agency is having a smart bash at The Connaught. And, well, I wondered if you would like to come?'

She was so surprised that she audibly gasped down the phone.

'What as one of Derek Henderson's cast-offs! Is that what you do — pass your girlfriends around when you're tired of them? Go to hell!'

She slammed the phone down and stormed up to her room.

Two years later Mr and Mrs Winchester were inviting guests to:-

> *"The Wedding of their Daughter Vivienne to Mr. James Ward on Saturday May 25th at The Church of St. Peter, Berkhamsted."*

The day after she had slammed the phone down on him she had received a huge bunch of roses and a letter from Jim Ward. The letter had been apologetic, funny and persuasive (he was a copywriter, after all). Every day for a week, another bunch of roses, another clever and charming letter, and after seven days she was agonising over what to wear to the 'smart bash' at the Connaught'.

Jim wanted to invite Derek Henderson to the wedding, but made no protest when she objected.

But Jim and Derek remained friends, and when three years after their own wedding they were invited to Derek's she did agree to go.

Viv was oddly pleased to discover that the fiancee, Ursula, was not blonde.

Eleven years pass, and Jim is commuting from their postcard Cotswold cottage to an ad agency in Bristol, when Derek accepts a junior partnership in Gloucester, and once again Viv is thrown into Derek Henderson's company.

He and Ursula have chosen a large modern 'Prestige Residence' on a 'Prestige Gated Estate' just two miles from Jim and Viv's cottage. It boasts six bedrooms, a jacuzzi swimming pool, and mock Georgian pillars. Viv hates it.

But she no longer hates its owner. And she adores Ursula. Everyone adores Ursula — such a magnanimous host, such good company.

And Derek's letter? On his copy to her he had hastily scrawled 'be honest Viv!'

A sudden squall of wind and rain, tears the window off its catch, and she leaps up to pull it closed. It jerks her back from far away.

She gazes down at the paper in front of her:-

> '*Derek Henderson. Pros and Cons*'
> *Cons*
> *A self-satisfied shit!*

She folds the paper, tears it up and drops it into the rubbish bin under the sink.

****

'I don't know *what* to think, I really don't. Such a strange request. Are we supposed to take it seriously? It really is too inconsiderate, getting us all into a state....or am I making too much of it?......I expect I am....but can someone tell me what I am supposed to do?'

Julia, as always, is talking.

Graham and Martine Porter and Marcus and Julia Strickland are discussing Derek's letter, sitting at the card table in the elegant eighteenth century Drawing Room of the Stricklands' Grade One Listed Georgian mansion.

The great Sir Nikolaus Pevsner describes it as 'Handsome rather than Grand'; proportioned with Palladian elegance, four pilasters rising to Corinthian capitals astride a wide doorway with a delicate fanlight. The red brick Stables to the West of the house are also notable. This substantial Georgian Manor sits in eight hundred acres, which the present owners, Mr and Mrs Marcus Strickland, let as farmland.' The much thumbed Pevsner volume was strategically placed on one of the coffee tables, where it was difficult to overlook.

The Porters and the Stricklands play Bridge every month, taking it in turn to be host. A routine that the Porters rather regret, but in their American haste to be absorbed into the community, they had jumped at every invitation.

But it is amiable enough and they are very good listeners, a very necessary skill when Julia Strickland is within earshot.

Words race each other out of Julia's mouth, often colliding in their haste, and and the factory creating this verbal torrent is a model of productivity.

They were listening to Julia, now, but this time with some interest. Everyone had an opinion of Derek's letter, and were unselfishly happy to share it with anyone who would listen.

'When they first arrived Jim Ward was parading them around, rather like prize bulls, you know. I think he believed he had done us all a favour by introducing them into our midst. Ursula's mother, Lady Sedgwick, is the daughter of an Earl and her father is an Honourable,' and the tiniest hint of envy entered her voice. 'But, don't forget that Marcus' father was Sir Joseph Strickland, his father? No, his grand father I mean. Strickland jams were eaten at the highest tables in the land. We had the Royal Warrant you know.'

At which point Julia would usually race away for several minutes with a history of the Stricklands' family fortunes, a history with which her audience were usually more than familiar.

But on this occasion she had more pressing concerns.

'But, anyway, the point is, what are we going to do about Derek's letter? What am I supposed to say?'

'You work for the Citizens Advice Bureau', Marcus reminded her, 'writing evasive letters must be second nature to you', he laughed.

She had long since stopped hearing Marcus' niggling remarks.

'But what are we going to do, what are *you* going to do about his letter Graham? Martine?'

She stopped. She had surrendered the floor at last, but neither seemed in a hurry to take it.

'Are you going to answer it?' Julia persisted. 'I mean, I don't want to know what you would actually say, of course, but I mean, would you be very personal or just general?'

She stopped again. She was clearly anxious for their opinion. It was a position Graham and Martine had found themselves occupying all too rarely.

'I will answer it. Sure, I will', Martine said lightly. 'I'll say he's a nice guy, that I love him to bits, and I hope we'll go on being friends for a long time. Something like that.'

'Isn't that a bit - well - easy, Martine.'

'Sure Julia. But why make hard work of it?'

'I don't think I know him well enough to say I love him to bits', Julia said thoughtfully, and the other three laughed.

****

45

Dear Mr. Henderson

Your letter of 21st September
I thank you for your letter of the above date.

As Senior Clerk in the firm of Macklin Winter and Henderson you will forgive me if I say that I do not think it appropriate for me to offer any opinions on you as a person. Although I have never received anything but courtesy from you.

As employees — and I have been asked to represent the views, here, of all the non-partner members of the Firm — we are all agreed that you are a just employer. Quite firm when necessary, but never unreasonably so.

We have a high regard for your professional skills, if we may presume to say so, and find you unstinting with your time and advice when you believe we could benefit from it.

I hope — we all hope — that this reply is helpful.

Yours sincerely
The staff

****

Greta Davies read Derek's letter and snorted.

'Oh wad some power the giftie gie us
To see oursels as ithers see us.'

She read it aloud in a delightful lilting Swedish accent.

What on earth was it supposed to mean? Was it English?

She re-read the letter, and threw it angrily down on the table.

Derek Henderson had groped her one evening after a Christmas party at the Porters'. Earlier he had kissed her under the mistletoe, and she had kissed him back.

Wasn't that what you were supposed to do in England? Some silly old tradition.

Later he had grabbed her in the kitchen when she was doing some washing up, and pushed himself against her back, and reached round and put his hands on her breasts.

She had stamped back on his foot so hard that he had grunted in pain.

Neither of them had spoken of it since.

What was it about these Englishmen? Forever groping and smirking and flirting. Who said the English were slow to embrace foreigners?

They never stopped trying to embrace her.

Was it her fault? She wondered. Was she giving out all the wrong signals, or some special Swedish scent, like pinewood, that the male species couldn't resist?

Or the English male species.

In Sweden the boys had drooled over passionate dark Italian girls, or cool, elegant Parisians. Blue-eyed blondes were ten a penny in Stockholm.

She had yearned for the man who would sweep her off her feet, who would father her two, or maybe three, perfect children and build their dream house. On Lake Flaten, perhaps.

But then Peter Davies had walked into the travel agency on Klarabergsgatan, where Greta worked, and one year later they were divorced.

A whirlwind romance, a tempestuous marriage and a stormy parting. All Force 10.

He had yanked her out of Sweden like...well, pulling a swede from the garden, replanted her in a dreary basement flat in Swindon, and almost at once embarked on an affair with his secretary, a dumpy, flat-faced woman ten years his senior. So banal, so hurtful, so crushing for the lonely, homesick Greta.

Nevertheless she did not return to Stockholm after the rancorous divorce. She had been awarded the flat in Swindon and £55,000. She would stay in England.

A canny travel agent in Cheltenham had hired her, promoted her to Manager and then Partner in just three years. Her experience, her charm, her 'Swedishness' were great assets, and when a competitor tried to lure her away, the owner offered Greta 40% of the company to stay.

Greta had discovered the village with a keen stab of envy when delivering an expensive holiday itinerary to wealthy clients — Marcus and Julia Strickland.

She had waited two years before her ideal cottage came to the market, and she could finally shake suffocating Swindon out of her hair.

Now Greta picked up Derek's letter again, and read it again and tossed it down on the scrubbed pine table again. What a liberty!

She had half a mind to answer. 'Dear Derek, since you groped me at Martine's house I've found it difficult to like or respect you. But I can't be bothered to actively dislike you. Greta.'

Yes, she would send that.

****

Jim Ward sent an email to <danduhenderson@btinternet.co.uk>

Hi, Derek. Welcome back from the land of insights, to your home of expected insights — or slights, perhaps. God knows what I can say about you that I haven't said to you already over the years.

I first knew you as 'spotty' Henderson because you were spotty. Children are blunt about such things. Now that we are older we are not so direct. But if we were, what would we call you now? 'Cocky' Henderson? 'Generous' Henderson? 'Impatient' Henderson? 'Hard-working' Henderson? 'Provocative' Henderson? 'Clever' Henderson? 'Good Friend' Henderson?

Something of all those, I suppose. And perhaps now we should add 'daring' Henderson. Or 'crazy' Henderson, to send the letter you did. I hope it turns out a worthwhile exercise for you. That it makes you into a 'wise' Henderson.

And I wonder if you will share with us the results of your survey!

'Dying-to-find-out' Ward

****

The Gloucester Daily Times, September 24th
LOCAL MAN DEMANDS THE TRUTH, THE WHOLE TRUTH, AND NOTHING BUT THE TRUTH.

Penelope Draper

Is this bravery? Is it wise? Judge for yourself.

Yesterday, this paper received from an anonymous reader a letter he/she had been sent on Monday. He/she thought it might interest our readers, and it certainly intrigued us. Our anonymous correspondent has erased his or her name, but it was clearly sent to more than one person - perhaps many.

It was written by a Mr. Derek Henderson, a local man from Winchcombe, who wants to know exactly what people think of him.

Inspired, apparently, by Robbie Burns who suggests we would all benefit if we saw ourselves as other people see us, Mr. Henderson has invited our anonymous reader to furnish him with a very detailed criticism of all his faults and strengths.

Now, this paper is as ardent as any in its restless search for truth, so we have to respect Mr. Henderson's desire to find it — even if the search is rather self-centred. But surely some truths are better not probed too deeply.

Modestly, Mr Henderson compares himself to Charles Darwin. Like the great naturalist, Mr Henderson hopes to find great insights while away in the Galapegos islands, where he is currently on holiday. But unlike Darwin, who was so important to our understanding of evolution, our inquisitive gentleman from Winchcombe is only interested in discovering something that might benefit himself. Or not. Suppose he learns that most of his 'friends' don't much like him or don't trust him, or worse still find him deadly dull.

But what do you think? Would you be prepared to put yourself under the microscope with your workmates or playmates?

Write and tell me what you would like to tell Mr Henderson, and we'll publish the best of them.

You can read Mr. Henderson's letter on our website.

Letters to The Editor

That bloke in Winchcombe Henderson who wants to know what peeple think of him well Ill tell you hes a b***** idiot (This unsigned letter in response to Penelope Draper's article (24th September) is not untypical of several we have received that are less than complimentary to Mr Henderson - but more thoughtfully and grammatically expressed. Editor)

Sir,

I do object to the tone of Penelope Draper's article (Sept. 24) about a private letter that was sent by Derek Henderson to a group of his friends and family. He did not send it for publication, and I don't know if you had any right to publish it. The article was clearly showing bias in its content, and in my view poor judgment. I am a friend of Derek Henderson, and I can tell you that he's a kind man, with a great sense of humour and a very enquiring mind — that much is clear from his letter. I think what he has done is both interesting and brave. Hats off to him.

Yours sincerely
Peter Dobson
PS. It's The Galapagos Islands not The Galapegos Islands. Another example of a poorly considered article.

Dear Ms Draper

I thought your article (September 24th, Ed) about that man in Winchcombe who wanted to know what people thought about him, showed just what a self-centred, vain, and as you said, deadly dull man he must be. A woman would never lay herself open to such ridicule.

Agatha Barnes

This correspondence is now closed. Editor

Bruce Macklin wrote to Derek Henderson, his partner, on the firm's headed paper.

He typed it himself. It was not, he considered, for a secretary's eyes.

Dear Derek

I am writing concerning your letter of 21st September.

As you know, when Dennis Winter and I offered you a junior partnership, and later a senior partnership in this firm, we were very happy that you accepted.

And to date we have been more than happy with the contribution you have made to the partnership. You have brought us new ideas, and, more important, new clients.

It would be most unfortunate if that good work were to be undone by a professional misjudgment. I refer to the letter mentioned above.

Perhaps you do not know, but while you were away in South America, your 'open' letter found its way into the columns of The Gloucester Daily Times. It is disappointing that such a trivial — forgive me for so putting it — letter should be considered worthy of inclusion into the local newspaper, but it did excite comment both in the paper itself and from several correspondents.

Unfortunately, it also excited comment from some of this firm's clients, and not, I must tell you, very favourable comment. One of your biggest clients, indeed, expressed the worry that someone who was in charge of his affairs could show such dubious judgment as to lay himself 'open to ridicule' as one letter to the paper put it.

Dennis Winter and I believe it would be in the firm's and

all our interests if on your return to these shores, you write another letter to all our clients to mollify the concerns that were caused by the first one.

We would be be very happy for you to draft that letter, of course, but we both feel that it would not be unreasonable for us to see it before it was despatched.

Macklin, Winter and Henderson has some serious reassuring to do.

Yours sincerely
Bruce Macklin.

Senior Partner, Macklin, Winter and Henderson

****

These were some of the reactions sparked by Derek Henderson's letter, awaiting the author's return from South America. Will he be even less of a Robbie Burns fan when he reads all the other responses?

PARADISE LOST

An unfamiliar disease can cause chaos amongst an isolated people.

And poor isolated Horace Eastham was struck down by a disease he had no experience of, no resistance to, and so its symptoms were all the more acute.

Heartache, exhilaration, hope, yearning and dismay.

More precisely, Greta, as in 'better', Davies.

Horace had been quite unable to sleep after he returned from the Stricklands' party.

It was his habit when arriving home from a rare social visit to grab a book and read a few chapters, to expunge the tiresome occasion before he went to bed.

But on that night he had not even glanced at his book. He had flopped down in his shabby armchair, seeing nothing but Greta Davies and she listening to him so attentively.

How he had talked! How he had relished talking to this lovely understanding lady. 'How he had relished talking'. The very notion was astounding. It was so unlike him. It was so…liberating. A gag had been ripped from his mouth, and nothing would stop him from talking to the Greta in his head. Oh, he had so much to say, so many thoughts to share, his spinning mind just could not rest.

And the hours passed and the dawn came and still he was talking to Greta. And she, of course, was listening in rapt attention and with obvious sympathy.

And finally he slumped to sleep in his chair, and woke to a wet Sunday morning, raindrops running down the window panes, dribble running down his chin and the overwhelming feeling that he had found a soulmate.

He had shared so much with Greta Davies the night before, the bond had seemed so strong that he felt she, in turn, had shared so much with him.

But although they had talked earnestly for most of the evening, he was surprised to find how little he knew about her.

Was she married? He didn't know. Did she live locally? How did she know the Stricklands? Did she have children? Or a career? He had no idea.

She was from Stockholm, and was called Greta Davies. He remembered that, and she was very pretty, very blonde, he couldn't forget that. But that's all.

'Did I talk about myself, too much?' he wondered with a spasm of worry.

'Did I make a fool of myself?' another spasm.

But no, he saw her face, smiling, encouraging, listening with such eagerness, such sympathy. He just had to see her again.

It was two-thirty before the caterers had tidied up after the party and left — and Marcus and Julia Strickland were enjoying a late leisurely breakfast, the Sunday papers spread before them, when the doorbell rang.

Marcus raised his eyebrows at Julia who shrugged her shoulders. The door bell was rung again, with more urgency.

'Well aren't you going to answer it?' Julia asked.

'That's what we pay Maria for.'

'Who, as you very well know, is at her brother's wedding in Madrid.'

Marcus sighed and left the room and after some mumbled conversation in the hall, returned with Horace Eastham.

'Horace!' Julia's amazement was transparent. Any visit from Horace was unprecedented. His rent was paid into their bank account, exactly to the day, any requests or problems with the flat arrived by letter. But for him to walk in unannounced, and on a Sunday morning, well ...!

Horace's embarrassment was transparent, too.

'Oh, you're eating. I'm sorry. I should have... I didn't know it was so early. I'll come back later', and he started to back out of the room as if Marcus was the very king to whom his grandfather had supplied marmalade.

Marcus urged him back. 'It's not early, Horace, we're late. The party went on a bit.'

And Julia added, 'Do come in Horace, excuse the dressing gowns. Come and have some coffee.'

Horace hesitated, but then, overcoming his instinct to flee, moved with many apologies to the table and perched on the very edge of a chair.

'Did you enjoy the party, Horace?' Julia asked. Like everybody else she had been astonished to see Horace in such deep conversation with Greta.

'The party? Yes I enjoyed it. Very much.'

'I did see that you were rather monopolising Greta Davies, depriving all the men of her ...' she would like to have said outrageous flirting, but settled for...'Swedish charm.'

'Yes, Greta.' He stared at his coffee cup, fiddling and fiddling with the spoon in the saucer — 'clink, clink clink.' Julia resisted the urge to reach over and take it from him.

'I have a book she wanted to read, but I don't know how to reach her, where she lives.' Horace said in a rush, which to Marcus and Julia sounded much rehearsed.

If Horace had overcome all his debilitating shyness to burst in on them like this, he must have been well and truly bowled over by the woman. 'Poor sap', Julia thought.

Should she warn him? Should she tell him that Greta Davies was a nasty piece of work, forever trying to seduce every man in the neighbourhood, including her Marcus. Should she tell him that she had married an Englishman, probably for his citizenship, and ditched him after just one year, taking most of his money.

What hope would the innocent Horace have with such a dangerous woman?

Julia's hostility towards Greta was deep. And perhaps even she couldn't say why.

Marcus broke into her thoughts. 'Greta lives in one of the cottages just beyond The Black Horse, I've got her telephone number somewhere. I'll dig it out for you.' He got up and left the room.

'Did you know that Greta Davies was married, Horace? Not for long. She divorced her husband after just one year, but kept his money.' Why had Marcus that woman's telephone number?

Horace turned the spoon over and over in his saucer —'clink, clink clink' — but said nothing.

Marcus returned with Greta's address and telephone number and Horace, muttering more apologies, left.

'And why have you got Greta Davies' telephone number, may I ask?' Julia accused him.

'She gave us her card when we were planning the trip to Burma.' Greta managed a travel agency in Cheltenham.

'Oh.' Julia almost sounded disappointed.

Horace rang Greta as soon as he got back to his flat. Such decisiveness was again untypical, but today was not yesterday, nor all the yesterdays that stretched fainter and fainter back to his beginning. And, besides, he also sensed that if he delayed the call now, he might never have the courage to make it.

The 'phone rang and rang and rang and rang and rang and rang and ra-----

'Hello, Greta Davies.' Just hearing the voice, just hearing the name!

'It's Horace Eastham. We met at the Stricklands' party last night. We talked rather a lot.'

'Well you certainly did' she laughed.

'I talked too much didn't I?' Yes, thought Greta. 'No' she said 'I was interested.'

'There's so much more I would like to say.' he blurted out.

Oh dear. Greta didn't like the sound of that. She had heard quite enough about Horace Eastham already.

'Well...' she couldn't find the right words, and her head was aching. She had drunk too many glasses of wine to relieve the monotony of his endless confessional.

There was a long silence.

'Hello?' Horace spoke first.

'Yes, I'm still here.' she said.

'I wondered if'... there was a pause. What did he wonder, she thought 'I wondered if you would like to have some tea one afternoon.'

'Tea?' Not a proposition that Greta Davis was accustomed to.

'I can usually get away from Pate's by four, and there's a tea shop quite close. I am informed that their buns are very good.'

'You like nice buns, do you, Horace?' She kicked herself the moment the words left her mouth, but, of course, he missed the innuendo.

'Well, I don't eat many, but I liked them as a boy.'

There was another silence. She was not helping him one little bit, she knew, but she had encouraged the man quite enough last night.

'So' she could sense his struggle, poor man 'do you think you would like to have some tea, one afternoon?'

And she relented a little. 'Alright, I will have some tea with you, one day. But I don't know when. I'm very busy at work right now.'

'You work. I didn't realise, I'm sorry.'

This was getting awkward. 'I have to go now, Horace, I'm going out to lunch', she lied. 'Why don't you ring me in a couple of weeks or so, and perhaps we can arrange tea together.'

'Yes, I will.' He said eagerly. And they rang off.

He was very happy that she had agreed to meet again, and hoped he hadn't been too pushy.

She just sighed.

He was waiting for Greta in the tea shop with the nice sticky buns.

It was five weeks and three days since he had met her at The Stricklands' party and on every one of those thirty eight days he had thought about Greta at inordinate length.

He had tried four times to fix this meeting, and was beginning to wonder if he had misjudged the situation

...her interest in him ...her sympathy for him, when she had finally agreed on a day.

Since when he had been in a state of high anxiety. Suppose she didn't come. And if she did, what should he say? Yes, he had so much to say, but how should he start? And how could he stop himself talking too much? He must listen to Greta. He must ask her about herself. He saw her pretty face, and wondered what she would see. He looked in the mirror and turned quickly away from the gaunt, anxious face that stared back at him.

They had fixed to meet at four o'clock, but Horace had arrived at the tea shop soon after 3.30pm. Suppose she came early and he wasn't there, and she went away. He sat stiffly on the hard oak chair and stared at the door like a faithful dog left outside a shop.

The waitress had been one of his pupils at Pate's, and she was surprised he hadn't recognised her. He was well known for his photographic recall of all his ex-students. But today he looked sort of —well, odd.

Greta, anxious to dampen his expectations of the meeting, arrived deliberately late , but his expectations were not dampened in the least degree.

His heart beat wildly as she hurried to his table, full of apologies and animation and prettiness.

'What a day!' She was taking off her coat, looking for a hook to hang it on 'sorry I'm late Horace. I hope you haven't been waiting too long'. She found a hook, 'this looks a nice place. It's quaint, isn't that what you say in England?'

She sat down and threw her golden hair away from her eyes. 'Well, here we are and I'm starving. I can't wait to get one of those buns you promised.'

She gave him a smile designed to put him at ease but turned his stomach into knots.

'Well, how are you Horace?'

Horace studied her earnestly. A question so innocuous to anyone else, was to Horace a real conundrum. He was determined not to hog the conversation, he must ask Greta the many questions that he had failed to ask before, the many questions that he had rehearsed and rehearsed in his head since. Yet, at once, here she was encouraging him to talk about himself. 'How are you, Horace?' The same friendly smile, the same sympathy in her voice.

'Well', he said with deliberation, 'I am not sure how I am, Greta. I have been wondering about that a great deal since we met. Until then, I never believed there was anything to say about me. Who I was or how I was — those concepts meant nothing. But when I met you the dam burst, and it all came flooding out. And it didn't stop when you left. I went home and talked and talked to you in my head, most of the night. I didn't want to stop talking to you. And I suppose I still don't. I want you to know everything about me. I want to know everything about you.'

Greta listened to this response to her innocent question with equal measures of alarm and admiration. It was so rare to meet such transparency, such honesty in anyone, let alone a man. He was so vulnerable. He needed protecting.

But not by Greta Davies, thank you!

It was her own fault, she knew that. She had egged him on, mercilessly. She had used all her charm and feigned interest to open him up like a rusty tin trunk found in an attic. It had been a struggle but she had triumphed. Only to find there was nothing inside that she wanted to keep. He had 'phoned her the next morning and four times since and she had been cool and discouraging. She had only come to the tea shop to say ' It was nice to meet you, Horace. But goodbye', but he wasn't making it any easier.

'What can I get you, sir?' At last the waitress with her pad.

Horace glanced at her then smiled. 'Why hello it's Patty Wenman isn't it? Excellent French and History A levels. Were you not going up to Durham?'

'Warwick, sir. Next September, I'm taking a gap year, first.'

'As a waitress?'

'Only until I've earned enough to go to Nicaragua with Raleigh International as a volunteer.'

'Well good for you.'

When Patty Wenman left Greta remarked how naturally and easily he had talked to her. 'Well, of course,' he said with some surprise, 'I am a teacher.'

'And you are an adult, but you have some difficulty, I believe, talking to other adults.'

'Except you, Greta.'

'OK, let's talk about that. I'll try and be honest — for once.' She took a deep breath.

'When I saw you at the Stricklands' standing terrified behind the piano, I thought of you as a challenge. I'd heard you were like a snail hiding in its shell.'

'All smothered up in shade'. He quoted, and seeing her blank look added 'Shakespeare.'

'Anyway, so I set out deliberately to coax you out, to get you to talk to me. To win you over, I suppose. It wasn't very kind of me and I'm sorry I did it.'

'Don't be sorry, Greta' he implored, 'please don't be sorry.' He moved his hand as if to hold hers, but she moved it smartly away. 'I can't tell you how happy I am that you winkled me out of my shell. I can't tell you how much I was looking forward to this afternoon. I think you're wonderful, Greta.'

'Oh dear. This isn't going to be easy.' She sighed. 'Don't say that. Don't say anything. Look here are the cakes, which will you have?'

While Greta pondered over the cakes on Patty's trolley, Patty pondered over Horace. Mr.Eastham with a woman! A sexy blonde woman. Weird.

As the trolley trundled away, Greta looked into the anxious eyes of the awkward schoolmaster opposite her.

Would it hurt her to indulge him just a little? Let him talk to her, as he wanted, once in a while? But where would that end? Wouldn't he get more and more serious about her? And then she would hurt him more. Oh dear, the poor man.

She bit into her cake. It wasn't fresh. 'How is it? The cake?' he asked eagerly.

'It's very nice'. She lied.

He looked ridiculously pleased.

'I would like to know so much about you.' He said. 'Julia Strickland told me you have been married. And you have a job, but I don't know what it is. Do you have children? Do you like the opera? I read a good deal, do you? Do you like butterflies? Do you —'

'Whoa!' Greta held up her hands, and laughed. 'OK. Yes I was married to an Englishman —hence the Davies — my Swedish name was Lindgren, Greta Lindgren. The marriage was not a success, and, no, we were not blessed — thank God — with children. I run a travel agency in Cheltenham. I don't know if I like opera, and I read a lot - but not the kind of books you read, I'm sure. What else was it? Oh butterflies. I can't imagine anyone not liking butterflies, can you?'

'I used to collect butterflies and moths and pin them to a board.' He said seriously. 'and beetles and birds eggs and insects and orchids and flowers. I have quite a collection.'

'Naughty boy', she chided him, 'aren't you supposed to leave things growing in the wild?' He appeared to have forgotten he had told her about his collection at the Stricklands' party.

'Oh, I was just a child. Not a very happy child. I had no brothers...' ,and he was away.

Greta's heart sank as he began, again, the long recital she had listened to with growing boredom at the party.

It was too much.

'Horace, I'm going to stop you, right there. I am very sorry, but I do not want to hear about your childhood again. Or your school or University, or your teaching again. I don't want to hurt you. I really don't. But, Horace I don't believe we have very much in common.'

'Oh, I see.' He looked completely crushed.

'I have never met anyone like you before, and I mean that as a compliment. But you're so different to me — and I am sure very much kinder, more interesting and nicer than me — that you must stop thinking of me as special, if you do —'

'Yes, I do. Very special.' He blurted out, loudly enough to attract Patty's and the other customers' attention.

'Well I am not.' She said quietly to encourage him to lower his voice, too. 'I'm not special. I'm not clever. I'm not interesting. I'm middle aged and middle brow and predictable. And I don't like change.'

As Greta trotted out this list of shortcomings to lower Horace's opinion of her, she was painfully aware of the truth of the self-assessment.

Horace, whose head had been so full of thoughts to share with this wonderful woman, could now not think of a single word.

The silence stretched and stretched and he yearned for his crib sheet.

Eventually Greta said quietly, looking at the unhappy man who was staring at his plate, 'Horace, thank you for being so honest. Thank you for trusting me. I am truly sorry.'

She got up, slipped a five pound note onto the table for her tea, collected her coat and left the cafe.

Horace sat looking at the empty chair for so long that Patty Wenman was getting concerned, when he suddenly rose and left.

The five pounds did not cover the cost, but Patty paid the difference out of her own purse.

TAPED

'My God, can that woman talk!' Brian grumbled, slouched in the passenger seat, feet on the dashboard. 'At least you could dull the pain, with alcohol.' Marcia snapped. 'It's high time you did your share of the driving.' He appeared not to hear.

'Her epic saga of the day her 'fridge conked out must have taken half an hour.'

'Don't be silly.'

'Well, It felt like it.'

'Did you hear what I said about the driving, Brian?'

'I did, and I do. I drove on Tuesday night.'

'Yes, when we visited your teetotal parents.'

Once again Brian stalled. 'But, I ask you, how can a simple story about a refrigerator take in her three years at college, the first time she met Marcus, her aunt's appendicitis, the road that's being dug up in Bourton, the---'

'I don't want a replay, Brian.' Brian stared ahead as the headlights lit and then lost the familiar, twisting country lane. 'Actually,' he mused, 'Julia's stories are not without a certain fascination — as long as you don't expect them to end. Does she, herself, believe that there's any thread of logic or direction in them? As she zigzags from one stream of consciousness to the next, from one sudden memory to another, does she ever expect to get back to the bloody fridge where it all started?'

'She's a social worker. Probably has to spend most of her time listening —'

'She should listen to herself, sometime —'

'So when she can talk, she does.'

'And how!' The car pulled into their cottage driveway.

'You're too critical Brian. Julia's a very generous and kind person.' She waited while Brian swung open the garage door, drove in and parked her Prius next to Brian's cherished Bentley and switched off. But Brian wouldn't let it rest. While Marcia poured herself a generous glass of wine, he whined on. 'You know I wouldn't mind recording one of Julia's stories — I think a psychiatrist, or maybe a sociologist, would be genuinely interested to hear one.'

'You make her sound doolally.'

'You said it. I hope she makes more sense at the Citizen's Advice Bureau. There must be some mighty confused citizens around here.'

'Come on Squidge.' Marcia shooed the cat off the sofa and out into the kitchen.

'It's time we had Julia and Marcus over for a meal, we've been there twice since they've been here.' She called from the kitchen

'Oh Lord, do we have to?'

'Yes, we do. And Ian and Deborah, and Derek and Ursula and maybe Jim and Viv, too.'

'I suppose so', Brian reluctantly conceded.

'Just think, you could record one of Julia's stories.' Marcia was joking.

'Well, yes, that's true!' Brian wasn't. 'So I could.'

Marcia came back from the kitchen. 'Don't you dare, Brian. I can't believe that you could even *think* of spying on our friends. Anyway, I'm going to bed, can you do the alarm?'

'Sure. I'll be up in a second' Brian said thoughtfully. But he wasn't thinking about the alarm and what he *was* thinking would certainly have set alarm bells ringing for Marcia.

Brian was going to do a bit of spying.

Unlike 007, Brian had no 'Q' to supply him with devilishly cunning equipment, so had to resort to the next best thing — Google.

He typed in 'recording devices', and clicked. The first page he opened began with a solemn warning that any surreptitious recording of any electronic, telephone or oral communication was a federal offence in the US, punishable by up to five years imprisonment. Brian, somewhat alarmed, tried 'recording devices UK', and opened a very pandora's box of sneaky equipment. He found lipstick recorders, a spaghetti telescope and a drinks can telescope, an ultra violet pen light with message shredder, an ear spy ('Fun for kids but can be used by adults, too'). Page after page, from the tiny – 1 cm square – to bulky briefcase recorders and telephone taps. Nor were there dire warnings of the consequences of using them. Brian whistled through his teeth. It seemed that snooping on your enemies, and colleagues and even friends was big business.

But, he reasoned, he wouldn't be spying on Julia. Spying was obtaining information not meant for your eyes or ears. And Julia was hiding nothing - on the contrary she was desperate to be heard. No, it wasn't spying, just recording for posterity. It sounded better like that.

All the same he was far from sure of the wisdom of taping Julia Strickland. How could he possibly use it? And he could never tell Marcia. He was on the point of aborting his search when he stumbled on the ideal device. It was a slim, small transmitter, 'no bigger than a AAA battery' that could be taped to the underside of a chair or table and transmit to a recorder hidden up to 40 feet away. 'Will record for up to six hours! Just £49.95 including VAT and postage!' the ad boasted.

Brian gazed out at the Cotswold hills which rose so smoothly beyond the end of his garden and paddock. A kestrel hovered high over the sheep shorn grass, and he waited for it to swoop down for a dramatic kill, but it wheeled away and flew out of his sight. Brian turned back to his computer hovered for a moment then swooped onto the keyboard and ordered the transmitter and recorder, with a frisson of excitement.

The excitement soon gave way to worry. If it really was an offence to record a conversation surreptitiously he had just bought some equipment that could be used for illegal purposes. Moreover he had given his name and address, not to mention his credit card details, to some unknown Company that for all he knew was as questionable as the products it sold.

'Bloody fool.' He muttered.

Could he be blackmailed? Could he be traced by the police? In the event, the parcel arrived the very next day and was waiting on the hall table when Brian came in from work. There was nothing to identify the contents and Marcia didn't ask about it, though he had a story ready just in case. He went straight up to his study, closed the door, and examined the equipment. It was poorly made with a cheap plastic casing. Hmm — not very promising. Well, he would try it the next day, a Saturday, while Marcia was at her aerobics class in Charlton Kings.

The next morning, while Marcia twisted and stepped and stretched and sweated, Brian placed and tested his devices and replaced and retested them until he was happy he'd laid an ingenious Julia trap that would never be detected. All he needed now was a Julia to step into it.

And as soon as Marcia got home he asked if a date had been fixed for Ian and Deborah and the others to come to dinner. He was slicing an avocado for the salad he was preparing for lunch. A casual observer would have detected very little of the James Bond about Brian as he worked in a faded pink 'pinny' in their large old oak-beamed kitchen, with its warm terracotta floor tiles and Persian rugs. But Marcia was not a casual observer - not of Brian Woodrow, anyway.

She took a long swig from her bottle of Evian, and studied her husband very deliberately. 'It's not like you to show interest in planning a supper.'

But he'd thought that through. 'I rang Ian when you were out, to fix up a game of golf next week. He said they wanted to ask us round for a meal, and I said 'snap!' OK?'

'Hmm.' Marcia picked up her trainers and went off for a shower. She called back from the stairs ' So when did you arrange to play golf?'

'We couldn't find a day. I'll put the Quiche in the oven in ten minutes, which gives you half an hour.'

She didn't answer.

The wives couldn't find a day, either, when Marcia tried to arrange the supper, but finally, after the usual swapping and switching a date was fixed for a lunch four weeks later. 'Four weeks!' Brian was impatient, now, to lay his trap.

'Don't get paranoid, Brian. They could all do next Saturday, as it happens, but that's the day we're going to the Theatre in Cheltenham with the Andersons.'

'What are we going to see, remind me?'

'The magnificent Ambersons.'

Brian laughed 'I hope the Ambersons and the Andersons hit it off.'

As the lunch came closer Brian's resolve to record it weakened. How could he possibly use it? And if it backfired, if it was discovered... not good. Furious Marcia, indignant friends. Invitations dried up. But the chances of detection were negligible. He'd given it the Marcia test, with some trepidation, but she hadn't suspected a thing. And anyway he was enjoying the buzz. What an anti-climax if he stopped now. So on the day, while his friends were having a drink before lunch, he slipped into the dining room and switched on the recorder. The die was cast.

But the best laid plans. Julia never got out of first gear. There were openings, at which Julia duly leapt, but after a few random twists in her story Ursula Henderson would deftly slide into the monologue and take it on with such easy charm and good humour that Julia seemed quite unaware that she had been gently mugged. And, of course, everyone else was very much obliged to Ursula - except Brian.

His disreputable plan was being thwarted and he tried to give Julia openings himself. 'Tell them about that time your fridge conked out, Julia.' he prompted, to Marcia's undisguised astonishment. Julia leaped at the bait, like a half starved salmon. 'Oh yes, my goodness it certainly did! Do you remember Marcus? And at the worst possible time too, we were having friends to supper, the Linley's, you know James and Jessica

Linley, don't you Derek? Jessica Linley used to work with me at The Citizens Advice Bureau, but I first met her when Daniel, that was her son, was at primary school with Gillian. Of course when Gillian was accepted for Cheltenham Ladies College they rather last touch. I was quite pleased about that, because I don't think Daniel was a very good influence on her. He was nice enough but a bit rough round the edges and not terribly bright. Oddly enough Gillian seemed to be very attached to him. Well, anyway, we met them, again - that's James and Jessica - when we were staying with my parents in Tenterden, last Christmas. The Linley's were also down in Kent staying with friends over the holiday. You can imagine our surprise when they turned up at the carol concert in St Mildred's, they really do a wonderful carol concert there, you know. My mother does the flowers for the church and goes into the woods to collect all the holly she can lay her hands on, though it's really a private wood, but Colonel Dennis, who owns it, doesn't mind, he is a friend of my father, they met when they were on a shoot together in Yorkshire—'

In the mini-second when Julia took a breath Ursula saw her chance.

'Goodness, yes Julia! What is it about men and guns?' She beamed across at her. 'Daddy is just the same. Never happy unless he's shooting something. I don't think he really trusts anyone who can't bring down a grouse at 100 paces. Do you shoot Ian?' 'You must be joking. Me? The mass slaughter of beautiful wild birds like pheasants and grouse, just for the amusement of a few toffs!'

'Hold on, Ian.' Derek protested. 'Those birds wouldn't have any life at all if they hadn't been specially bred for the season. They have a wonderful six months with all the food they can eat and a very quick death, if they don't get clean away, which a good percentage do.'

'Well I agree with Ian.' Ursula said. 'Shooting is the middle class murder. It's no better than hoodies stabbing each other with knives.'

'Oh come off it, Ursula...' And like a twelve bore on the moors the debate went off with a bang.

Brian resigned himself to failure. Clearly he wasn't going to get a great Julia monologue on tape, so he settled back and enjoyed his friends' company and Marcia's cooking and filled his friends' glasses and refilled his friends' glasses and the conversation flowed with the wine. Derek was telling a rather good story when Marcia called from the other end of the table.

'Brian? Can you collect up the plates from your end, and give me a hand in the kitchen, please.'

'Sure.' He said, tearing himself rather reluctantly away. In the kitchen he got out the cheese, stirred the dressing into the salad, and started to fill the dishwasher while Marcia put the finishing touches to the raspberry Meringue pie and took the treacle tart from the oven.

'It seems to be going, OK.' Brian said. No answer.

'Don't you think?'

'Yes. It's certainly very noisy at your end of the table.'

'That's Derek, for you.'

'Poor Julia can hardly get a word in edgeways.'

'I noticed.'

'Aren't you pleased? You're always rabbiting on about her rabbiting on.' For once it was Brian who didn't answer.

It was almost six o'clock before the last of them tottered merrily towards their cars, and Brian started to clear up.

'Let's leave it.' Marcia said. 'I'll do it in the morning.' Marcia usually made this offer. Brian always refused it. It was a ritual. One day Brian thought he might call Marcia's bluff, but not today — today he had to get out the transmitter and recorder before Marcia discovered them. 'What a waste of time and money that was.' he thought as he hid them in a drawer of his desk.

And there they sat untouched for weeks. There was little reason to listen to them. But then one day when Marcia was out he *did* pull the recorder from the drawer and idly rewound the tape to the beginning and pressed PLAY. At first there was nothing but some very faint and indecipherable voices, and Brian supposed that the tape had not functioned properly.

'So much for the master spy' he thought. But then the voices grew clearer and louder, and he realised they were coming into the room. Marcia was asking him where the table plan was, then his voice 'Graham, you're here...Julia next to Graham...Derek at the end...' Brian pushed FAST FORWARD then listened again. A snatch of animated conversation, garbled whenever two or three people spoke at once. But it was an odd sensation. rewinding the occasion with such clarity.

He pressed FAST FORWARD, again and let the tape whizz through for some time, then PLAY, again. Just one voice this time, Julia's, talking very quietly, almost whispering. '...was having lunch at that expensive little restaurant in Winchcombe one day and they were there, too. My friend said that they looked ...well you know...*very very* intimate.'

Then Ursula's voice also kept very low. 'I do find that quite hard to believe, Julia. It just seems so... unlikely.'

'You women are incorrigible,' Graham laughing, 'but it does sound pretty intriguing.'

'Ssh. Keep your voice down Graham.' Martine hissed. Brian sat up and listened. Who were they gossiping about? He didn't remember this conversation, so it must have been when he and Marcia were in the kitchen sorting out the cheese and the puddings. And yes, at that point in the tape they can be heard coming back into the room, and there's a great to do, about Marcia's treacle tart and especially her raspberry meringue with almond cream.

'Just look at that! A work of art.'

'Oh, Marcia what are you doing to us?' And so on.

Brian stopped the tape and gazed, unseeing, over towards the hills. They had all been whispering. And the gossip had stopped abruptly when he and Marcia had returned. So they didn't want him and Marcia to hear. But what? They were all good friends. Surely there wasn't any scandal in the village they couldn't all share. It took several seconds for the penny to drop. 'Idiot!' He said aloud to the silent house. All he had to do was rewind the tape to the beginning of the whispering. It didn't take long to find it.

There was Marcia calling to him down the table to collect up the plates after the lamb tagine. And then much clattering and chattering as plates and cutlery were piled and ferried out to the kitchen. Their was a short silence, and then Julia said quietly, 'Well, they look happy enough.'

'Who?' Derek asked.

'Brian and Marcia.'

'Well why shouldn't they?' Derek again. And Brian sitting in his study all those weeks later repeated it aloud. 'Yes, why shouldn't they?' There was no answer on the tape from Julia. Then Ian 'Yes, why shouldn't they Julia? You seem to be suggesting something.'

'I don't like to spread gossip.' Julia whispering now.

'You could have fooled me.' Marcus, her husband. 'You know you're dying to tell us.'

'Well if you must know...' here Julia pauses, for effect... it's about Greta.'

'Greta!' says Graham. 'Are you suggesting that our naughty Nordic, and Brian are...how shall I put it, politely... having it off.'

'Honey, please!' hisses his wife.

'No, I am not suggesting that.' Julia sounds quite sure about that. 'Let's drop the subject, they'll be back soon.'

'You can't drop it, having thoroughly confused us.' Ian speaks for all, judging by the murmurs of agreement.

'Not Greta and *Brian!* ' Julia puts great emphasis on the 'Brian'.

There's a moment's silence on the tape, and Brian in his study thinks 'Greta and Marcia', but the words mean nothing. It's Ursula who says it on the tape. 'It sounds as though you're saying Greta and Marcia. You aren't saying that are you?'

'My god' says Derek 'what tosh!'

Julia, sounding stung, says 'Well, I hope you're right Derek. I can only say what I heard.'

'And that is?' Whispers Martine.

'That someone, who shall be nameless, was having lunch at that expensive little restaurant in Winchcombe one day, and they were there, too. My friend said they looked...well you know.... *very, very* intimate.' Brian switched off the tape. And sat for some time gazing at the recorder.

Then he shouted 'BLOODY COW!' Though who he meant was anybody's guess.

THE WOODROW AND THE WIDOW

Brian and Marcia Woodrow were introduced to Ian Hislop at The Cheltenham Literature Festival.

Of course they didn't flatter or fawn or, God forbid, ask for an autograph — no matter how often they had chuckled at his wit, no matter how avidly they had watched 'Have I Got News For You.' Any such one-sided admiration shown to a celebrity would suggest a lack of anything to celebrate about themselves....and, anyway, they wouldn't wish to embarrass him, would they? They and the Porters had just heard Hislop's presentation, and were shuffling out of the carpeted tent when Graham Porter noticed Douglas and Daphne Gunn talking to the very man who had just entertained them with such provocative wit.

'Come on,' he said with that shocking or liberating American indifference to social niceties, 'let's go say Hi to Hislop.' And Brian and Marcia followed their friends sheepishly to the table at the front.

'Ian,' Douglas Gunn said to Hislop, 'let me introduce

Graham and Martine Porter, friends from Pittsburg and now living near me in the village.'

'Hi, Ian.' Graham said, vigorously pumping Hislop's hand. 'That was a real fun talk. We loved it. And we love your TV show. And we can't wait to buy the book.' Far from embarrassed, Hislop beamed with pleasure. 'I'm very happy to hear it.' He said. 'Especially the last bit.'

'And I'm afraid I've forgotten your names.' Douglas Gunn said, turning to Brian and Marcia, and thus undermining their status in their own eyes if not Hislop's.

'Brian and Marcia Woodrow.' Brian said, shaking Hislop's hand. 'I'm the Brian bit.' Ian Hislop smiled wearily. It's the lot of the wit to attract facetious remarks.

'Ian Hislop,' he said, quite unnecessarily.

'And I'm Douglas Gunn.' Douglas said to Brian and Marcia, again unnecessarily, everybody in the village knew and admired the Gunns. 'And this is my wife, Daphne.' And that's how Brian Woodrow came to meet Daphne Gunn. An introduction that would prove to be far more significant than that to Ian Hislop. In his eyes, at least.

Douglas Gunn, OBE, was a distinguished QC with chambers in the Inner Temple, who sat as an occasional judge at the Bristol County Court. He was in great demand, and not just because he had happily discovered quite early in his career at the bar that the more he charged the more briefs he received.

He was tall and imposing — all the better for bearing down on the criminal classes and impressing wavering jurors and junior judges — and enviably successful at most tasks he set his mind to. His golf handicap was three. ('Haven't the time to get it any lower, I'm afraid.' he said). He'd played cricket for English schoolboys and a few times for a minor county. ('Until work would keep getting in the way.') And he had twice rowed for Oxford in The Boat Race. ('Won one, lost one. No draws.') Pleased with himself, yes, but not without reason. Ian Hislop, who was at Oxford with Gunn, had interviewed Douglas for his anarchic magazine called Passing Wind. The magazine was not generous to the university's ' Sporting Bores' as it labelled them, whose heads it suggested were far too big for the minimal braincells that were wandering around inside them. The article about Douglas dubbed him 'The Twelve Bore Gunn.'

For all that, Hislop and Gunn had got on well and had bumped into each over the years quite happily, most often in the Law Courts where both of them passed a good deal of time. Douglas Gunn building a formidable reputation, and Ian Hislop, as Editor of Private Eye, defending the outspoken magazine against a stream of litigation. Their meeting at Cheltenham, however, was brief. Ian Hislop was soon hurried away by a pretty young PR girl to a book signing and the Gunns, Porters and Woodrows stood around rather awkwardly until Graham suggested going for a bite to eat, and they found themselves 10 minutes later wedged round a small table at Pizza Express.

This gave Brian a long-awaited chance to study Daphne Gunn at close quarters — so close they nudged elbows as they struggled with their pizzas. He had first been aware of Daphne at a piano concert which she had organised and introduced in Stow-on-the-Wold. He had been hugely impressed. He told Marcia, as they drove home, how struck he had been by her easy manner and confident speech from the platform in front of 500 people. But he didn't tell Marcia how struck he had been by her long auburn hair wrapped around a lovely face that smiled with wide almond eyes and that night had shone with the pleasure of the music she was sharing with them all. 'Daphne Gunn.' He read from the programme, as Marcia scrambled eggs for a late supper.

'Is she anything to do with the Douglas Gunn at the golf club, I wonder?'

'Oh Brian! Daphne and Douglas moved down from London at least two years ago.'

'How come we haven't met them, then?'

'We have. They were at Graham Porter's forty-fifth birthday party, don't you remember? No you probably don't... the way you were attacking their Chateauneuf-du-Pape.' Brian ignored the barb. 'So where do they live?'

'On the way to Lower Slaughter, that beautiful Georgian house set back from the road.'

'He's a good golfer, plays off two or three. Way out of my league.'

Marcia wondered if Douglas Gunn wasn't out of Brian's league in more ways than the fairways, and then feeling guilty gave him a kiss as she put the eggs down in front of him. She wasn't to know that Brian was wishing that, in some ways, she was a little more like Daphne. More self-assured, more confident – more talkative, even.

'Perhaps we should have them over?' Brian suggested.

'Goodness. We hardly know them.'

But now they did. Her handshake had been firm, dry and warm. And here they were, huddled round a small table in high spirits. It was Friday night, the weekend beckoned, the Montepulciano was flowing and Brian was in good form. Marcia watched her husband with resignation. Of course he could be very amusing but he was clearly showing off to Daphne Gunn, and Daphne seemed to enjoy the attention. But if Douglas noticed Brian flirting with his wife he was far too self assured to show any sign of it. Graham, ever the spontaneous host, had insisted they all went back to his house for a drink, and the party continued there, Brian emboldened by the brandy to make longer eye-contact with Daphne than perhaps was polite.

A week or so later Brian was ordering a glass of wine at the golf club bar when Douglas had come over and spoken to him. A rare event; Douglas Gunn made little attempt to mix with other members, outside a few close friends — 'the pump-ups' as some of the less confident members oddly dubbed them.

'Hello Brian.' he said. 'It is Brian isn't it? Yes of course it is.'

'Hello. Can I get you a drink Douglas? It is Douglas isn't it? Yes of course it is.' Douglas laughed, accepted a white wine, and they stood at the bar talking easily about the golf club, Ian Hislop, the Cheltenham festival, the evening at the Porters' house.

'You were very entertaining.' Douglas remembered.

'You mean I talked too much. As my wife, Marcia, made crystal clear later.'

'Well my wife, Daphne, was quite impressed. You made a hit there. She tends to approve of creative types.'

'I'm only a graphic designer.' Nevertheless he was pleased and flattered that Daphne Gunn - the cool, attractive Daphne - approved. Very pleased.

Thirteen months later Douglas Gunn was dead. His Audi TTS Roadster skidded on a greasy bend and smashed into a tree as he was driving with his habitual urgency to a sitting at the County Court. The shock waves of his death were felt far beyond the village. Daphne and their children were inconsolable , of course, but his close friends and relatives were also distraught, and his many acquaintances deeply affected. And many others who had known him at school or university or in his early years at the Bar read the fulsome obituaries in the national newspapers and sent heartfelt condolences. Douglas Gunn was very much admired and very well liked. His memorial service at the Cathedral at Christ Church Oxford, the college where he had studied and sported with such distinction, was so well attended that many had to stand. Those thrilled to spot faces familiar to them through their newspapers or television sets were well rewarded — though not by Ian Hislop who was filming — and the tributes were both witty and very moving. The shock of his death, the waste of his life, was the all the greater for its brutal suddenness.

The service concluded, everybody moved to Tudor Hall, the college banqueting room, where a more temporal kind of refreshment was provided, and the mood visibly lightened. The buffet was lavish and the wine plentiful, and soon the whispering reverence of the Cathedral gave way to the noisy roar of a party. Old friends met and swapped their lives, relatives gathered in gossiping groups, the village crowd stuck together, and Derek Henderson amused them with a long story about a shooting party at which he hadn't bagged a single bird.

'Good for you.' Marcia said.

'Not at all,' Derek replied, 'it wasn't through lack of trying.'

Brian watched Daphne. She looked pale and drawn but she smiled gamely as she greeted dear friends, slight acquaintances and even total strangers who queued to express their sympathy. Brian could see the despair etched into her face. Poor woman - what an ordeal it must be. But to most of the others in that magnificent Hall, the worries, pleasures and needs of their own lives were, as ever, taking precedence. As Brian wandered around the room, refilling his plate and wine glass, he listened to the now animated chatter. If the death of a successful, charismatic and admired man like Douglas could affect, truly affect, people so little, how much impact would the death of someone like him, Brian, make? Especially as he had no children. 'Barely a bloody ripple,' he supposed. He recalled a French film, Huit Clos — was that the title? — where the dead stayed in a comfortable limbo until nobody in the living world was ever thinking or talking about them. Then they faded away. How long would he stay in that limbo?

'Come on Brian.' He was jerked from his morbid thoughts.

'We should be going. Graham and Martine are ready.' The Porters had driven them up to Oxford. 'But we must say goodbye to Daphne.' So they waited for their turn to tell Daphne, just as everyone else had, what a moving service it had been, and how sorry they were for her loss. And Marcia hugged her.

'Thank you so much for coming.' Daphne said, as she had to everyone else.

Daphne Gunn would happily have died herself, but the necessity of organising the funeral and the memorial service, of coming to grips with Douglas's numerous business affairs and of consoling her deeply affected children, kept the initial despair just below the surface. But at night it swamped her and only powerful prescription sleeping pills saw her through the blackest hours. Her friends in the village and beyond rallied round, inviting her into their homes, into their lives. Daphne was invited to more suppers, outings, theatres and even holidays than she had ever been when Douglas was alive. She accepted this kindness with gratitude, even though the happiness of her friends' marriages was a bitter reminder of the lost happiness of her own. But anything was better than sitting at home, sitting alone, sitting and remembering, remembering, remembering. Crying for Douglas yet furious with him for abandoning her in such a reckless manner. And that's how, many months later, she came to be having dinner with Brian Woodrow in a popular country pub. It was Marcia's idea.

Since the evening when they met at the Literature Festival, she and Daphne had become firm friends. They sweated and strained at the same Aerobics class at Charlton Kings, would go on shopping sprees to Bicester Village, and once or twice went up to a theatre matinee in London. These outings didn't include their husbands, and so Brian had few opportunities to impress or charm Daphne with his 'creativity'. But when Douglas died, and all thoughts of impressing or charming were inappropriate, he had too many chances. Marcia was particularly supportive to her grief stricken friend. Brian thought a little too supportive. They never went to the cinema or theatre or on a walk in the country or had a supper party without Daphne being asked, too.

'Anytime, Daphne,' Marcia said one evening, 'that you are in need of some company don't stand on ceremony just give us a ring and come over. Anytime at all. You're always welcome here. Isn't she Brian?'

'Of course.' He said, but perhaps not quickly enough, for Daphne said that she was sure Brian didn't want her under his feet all the time. And it was true. Brian, so attracted to Daphne initially, now found her difficult company. She was a woman of strong opinions, often at odds with his own, and Brian was irked by her intransigence, as she was no doubt, by his.

Marcia dubbed them 'the prickly pair'. Little by little he felt a growing and uncharitable irritation towards her which he just couldn't shrug off. Strangely, Marcia, to whom Brian was usually an open book, failed to detect his resentment. So when Daphne mentioned a new gastro-pub near Bourton and Brian showed interest, it was Marcia who made the date. 'Brian' she enthused 'you should take Daphne there. You know I'm not keen on pubs. Our reading group meets next Tuesday, you could go then.'

'Would you like to try it, Daphne?' Brian felt obliged to ask.

So the following Tuesday found them sitting in a Christmas-card old coaching Inn, at a small round table by the open fire, beneath the ancient beams, a candle flickering between them, and on the walls sepia pictures of an idyllic rural life long gone, but missed only in the abstract. It was awkward at first. Both were polite, and the conversation didn't falter, but nothing was said of much interest to either of them. Each avoided topics which they knew from experience agitated the other. He suggested a drink and she ordered a glass of white wine.

'Large or small?' The waitress asked, and Brian was surprised, but pleased, when she ordered a large glass. He hoped it might relax her. He hoped it might relax him, too, so he ordered the same, and when the starter arrived, their glasses now drained, he ordered a bottle, and slowly they both began to unwind. 'It's nice here.' Brian said looking around, then angry with himself. 'Nice! What an awful, lazy, unimaginative, catch-all word that is!'

'What is it then, if it isn't nice?' she wondered.

'Well, it's welcoming, homely, cosy, comfortable, relaxing... sort of 'nice', really.' He laughed.

'And are you relaxed?' she asked.

'Er, well I'm getting there.'

'That's the wine, I dare say.'

'Possibly.'

'I could see that you didn't want to come here with me.'

He thought about that.

'He's not denying it,' she said.

'I'm thinking about it. I suppose I did and I didn't. I was a little nervous as it happens.'

She ate a forkful of her steak before speaking.

'I liked your letter of condolence, Brian. Very much.' He was pleased. He had taken some time composing it.

'You'd be surprised how repetitive those letters can be,' she said. 'Kindly meant, of course, and I did appreciate them. But yours was different. It made me cry.'

'Oh God, I didn't mean to —'

'Don't worry. I cry all the time.' And as she spoke he saw tears forming in her eyes, two little almond pools.

'Sorry Brian, I shouldn't have said that.'

'Why on earth not?,' he asked.

'I don't want to burden anyone with my grief.'

'It might help to share it, Daphne.'

She looked at him, thoughtfully, for some seconds, and he wondered if she would accept his offer. Perhaps she needed a little push.

'I didn't know Douglas well,' he said, 'but I liked what I saw.'

'Everyone did, he was such a special person.' Her eyes filled with tears.

'Oh Brian, you can't imagine how desperately I miss him.' And the tears spilled over and ran down her cheeks.

'I'm sorry,' she said. Brian reached over and squeezed her hand. 'Don't be silly Daphne,' he said gently, 'tell me about him.'

At first he thought she wouldn't. She gazed miserably at the candle and almost blew it out with a heavy drawn out sigh, and then the dam burst and the words and tears flowed and he held her hand across the table and listened — and thought, again, how lovely she was.

Occasionally she would interrupt herself to say, 'Sorry Brian', dab at her eyes with a tissue, and peck at her food, and then start again with such an intensity, that the waitress held back before removing their plates. Perhaps she thought they were lovers patching up a quarrel, her in tears, him holding her hand. When Daphne had slowed down a little, Brian asked her how she and Douglas had met.

'At Oxford.' She smiled at a memory. 'I arrived with a scholarship and left with a First and a fiancee,' Douglas used to say. 'Not very modest, I suppose.'

'It sounds like he had plenty to be proud about.'

'Oh, he certainly did! His friends called him 'shooting star' or 'hot shot', partly because of his name, Gunn, of course — but mostly because he really was a shooting star. He rowed in the Boat Race twice, you know.' And when Brian nodded. 'Of course you do, you were at the memorial service. He was President of the Union, Assistant Editor of Isis...only the meanest in spirit didn't admire him.'

'And he admired you. Obviously.'

'I don't know why,' Daphne insisted, and Brian suppressed a smile.

'I was very earnest. Very wrapped up in my music and I suppose my politics. I was very left wing. Perhaps that was what interested Douglas. The attraction of opposites.'

'Nothing to do with your looks, of course.' Bad mistake. Daphne bridled immediately. 'I resent that, Brian. I'm sorry but I do. Some men can look beyond a pretty face, you know.'

'Of course they can. I'm sorry, Daphne.' She sighed sadly before admitting that she supposed she must have been have been 'quite attractive'.

'The students in my year voted me most likely to snare a rich or famous husband, and I knew they weren't thinking of my music or my politics. I was so angry. I hated the idea of being a sex object. I would have liked to have been voted as most likely to be prime minister or most likely to win a Booker prize'. But why are we talking about me?'

'I asked you how you met Douglas.'

'He came to a concert I was playing in.' Daphne gazed dreamily at the candle flickering between them.

'And afterwards a group of us went for a drink. He talked about the music and how much it had affected him, and we were still talking about Mozart and Hayden long after all the others had left.'

'I see,' Brian said. Smooth operator he thought.

'I supposed... no, I hoped...he might ask to see me again. But it was some weeks before I heard from him. I guess he'd been much too busy, but I was beginning to miss him. I used to speak to him in my head.'

A very smooth operator, Brian thought. Tears welled up again in Daphne's eyes.

'Oh, and how I miss him now! And this time he won't ring, however much I speak to him in my head.'

Daphne and Brian were the last to leave the pub, the last car to leave the car park.

When they arrived back at her handsome Georgian house, and Brian pulled up at the columned door, she sat gazing out of the windscreen, exhausted.

For an hour or so she had felt the relief of sharing her grief.

He started to say something about the evening but she interrupted him.

'Thank you Brian.'

'It was a pleasure, Daphne, more perhaps than I expected.'

'Not thank you for taking me to the pub. Not thank you for the meal. Not thank you for the wine.'

'You didn't like them?' he joked, but she didn't smile. 'Just thank you.'

She leant across and kissed him briefly on the cheek and was gone. He waited till she reached the house and stood silhouetted in the open doorway. She waved to him and then slowly shut the door. He sat there for a moment, then reached forward, switched on the ignition, started the car, put it into gear, released the handbrake and drove down the country lanes to the village and Marcia and home.

DRIVEN TO HOPE

Spare a thought for the son haunted by the success of a father.

And not the crushing success of a father familiar to millions through the pages and pictures of the press, but the success of a determined and sensible father who's business had earned the respect of his peers, a handsome lifestyle and the impatient envy of a son so anxious to make his mark in it.

Spare a thought for Ian Willard.

Both physically and fiscally his long awaited inheritance stands at a crossroads.

The car showrooms and service station built up so vigorously by his dad was now in danger of collapsing around him.

It was a stressful time and might explain, if not excuse, Ian's behaviour that spring. Behaviour he wouldn't have considered for a moment in easier days.

Ian had taken great pains to sketch out his site plans, and was less than amused at what he saw as Brian Woodrow's flippant response to his efforts.

In fact, Brian did try to look suitably serious when Ian spread the sheet of paper across the desk in his offices, but plainly his friend was no draughtsman.

'This is the site as as it now.' said Ian. 'These are the showrooms and office, these are the workshops.'

'Uh -huh.'

'This is the forecourt where dad had his famous Saturday car swaps.'

'God yes. They would bring Winchcombe to a standstill. But why did he stop them?'

'He didn't. I did, after he retired to Florida.' Ian said, somewhat defensively, Brian thought. 'They were a hell of a lot of work, and they were no longer bringing in enough punters.'

Brian said nothing.

'These are the petrol pumps, as you can see just six at the moment, and —'

'So that's what they are?' Brian couldn't resist. 'I thought they were martians.'

Ian glowered at him. 'Look, Brian, I don't pretend to be a bloody artist. That's why I've come to you, for Christ's sake.'

'You're right. I'm sorry.' Brian held up his hands. 'Go on.'

With a flourish Ian laid a second sheet of paper on top of the first.

'Now *this* is my grand new plan.' he said with enthusiasm. 'First, I want to put in four more... martians ... here.' Brian laughed out loud and Ian smirked, 'So I'll need a much bigger fuel storage tank, just here. The workshop stays as it is, but I want to increase the office and showroom by about 20%.'

'For your precious old cars.'

'Exactly, for my vintage cars. But the real change is here — the shop.' He prodded the paper with his finger, 'It has to be at least three times the size. A mini-supermarket, with large cold cabinets, a much wider range of foods, drinks, sandwiches, fresh breads, flowers, magazines the whole caboodle.' He looked at Brian searching for approval. 'So, what do you think?'

But Brian just couldn't bring himself to give his friend the unqualified thumbs up that was so obviously expected.

'It looks very ambitious Ian. But will the District Council give it the nod? Beautiful Winchcombe being beautiful Winchcombe.'

'Yes, well, I'm counting on your equally beautiful drawings to win them over. But, seriously, they better go for it, or very soon Willard's will be out of business. After 69 years.'

'As bad as that! You told me BP was undercutting your petrol prices, but going out of business...'

'It's not just the petrol, it's their bloody great store. You've seen it, and how busy it gets. It's sucking away some of my oldest customers.'

Brian, who had himself occasionally been sucked away, just nodded.

'No, If I want to compete, to win back my old customers, I've got to match that BP site. It's a hell of a gamble, I know that, and Debbie's worried sick about it — I know that, too — but I can't go down without a fight. Dad would turn in his grave.'

Brian appeared to study the plan, but was thinking about his friend. Was Ian really the David to take on a gigantic global Goliath?

His father might have pulled it off, but his father had been aggressive, charming, determined and cunning. Ian was merely charming and quite hard working. And where was the money to come from? He suspected that his friend was already struggling.

'It's not going to be cheap!' he said.

'Fifty thousand. Sixty, at the most.' Ian said, confidently.

Brian would have guessed more, but presumably Ian had done the sums.

'You need a windfall, Ian.'

'Yes, well, I can't see any ripe apples about to drop into my lap.'

'Didn't I hear Marcus Strickland telling you that he had some old wreck under dust sheets in his stables?'

Ian flicked the remark aside. 'This is what my livelihood depends on, Brian,' again prodding his plans, 'not finding old wrecks. I've been on a good few wild-goose chases over the years after 'tip-offs' about old cars.'

'I can imagine. But think of all the money sloshing around that family. Remember Strickland jams?'

'How can we ever forget with Julia to remind us? Now let's talk about these plans. I want one of your clever fellows to work some real magic on them. And no cost spared, Brian, a lot hangs on them.'

Well, we'll see about that. The cost, I mean. And, don't worry, I am sure we can make the new Willard's look impressive.'

It was 1947.

Jack Willard, 28, and impatient to make up for the years lost in the war, was searching for opportunities in the Cotswolds, criss-crossing the country on his BSA 250 motorbike, when he came across the derelict site on a road junction near Winchcombe.

He coasted onto the cracked concrete forecourt, switched off the engine, yanked his bike onto its stand

and walked around the broken buildings. The fallen roofs, the rotting woodwork, the smashed windows, shrubs were growing through the concrete, piles of stinking litter tipped everywhere.

It was perfect.

Sergeant Jack Willard had spent the war patching up tanks and lorries, and now in this abandoned workshop he intended to patch up the cars of post war Britain.

The farmer who owned the land was only too happy to be rid of the eyesore, and Jack snapped up the two acre site for £375.

His vision and his timing were impeccable.

The demand for cheap cars after six austere years of war was irresistible, and the creaking British motor industry, hobbled by antiquated machinery and bloody-minded unions rushed out one poorly made model after another that were forever struggling into Jack's workshop for repairs and attention.

By the time Bill Hailey was rocking around the clock, Jack Willard and his growing team were working round the clock and by the time Beatlemania brought America to its knees, he was president of the Rotary Club and a District Councillor.

To nobody's surprise, his fellow councillors unanimously approved his application to add petrol pumps, a car showroom and an office to his workshop.

And to nobody's surprise Jack resigned as a councillor soon after, citing his increased workload.

The Council had served its purpose.

By 1969 he could afford to buy one of the very first, and very desirable, Aston Martin DBS V8s and to send his son, Ian, to an expensive private boarding school.

The Aston Martin was the better investment.

Ian was a reluctant and indifferent pupil - english and chemistry could never compete with his passion for engines and cars. His school books were filled with sketches of Bugattis and Alfas, his head crammed with an encyclopaedic knowledge of every classic car from the very first Benz of 1886.

The very day after he left school, with just four O levels, he joined his Dad at Willard's, but the apostrophe on the large painted nameplate over the showroom stayed firmly where it was — there was never any doubt who was running the show.

Nevertheless Ian did persuade his father to give him part of the showroom to sell older models which he bought and restored. He called it, somewhat euphemistically, Vintage Corner.

It seldom produced the income to justify the expense, but Jack enjoyed indulging him. He was proud to have his son working alongside him, teaching him the trade and the tricks of it, how to balance the books, how to sweet talk a sale.

'We're not a bad team, son.' He would say.

'Sure Dad.' Ian would reply, as he was expected to. But deep down as year followed year he began to believe, like so many sons in family firms, that his father was holding them back.

He wasn't receptive to Ian's big ideas for the business. He missed opportunities that Ian suggested. He, Ian, could run it so much better, if only he had the chance, he believed.

And finally in 1994 it came.

Jack retired and he and wife Betty moved to Florida.

'It's just such a pity it's so far,' Deborah said. She put great store in her father-in-law's advice.

'Not at all. He's out of interference range.' Ian had replied.

At last *his* ideas would drive the business. *His* hands were on the steering wheel.

It wasn't altogether Ian's fault that his stewardship of Willard's coincided with a remorseless decline in profits. But he knew he would be judged against his father and it was becoming an obsession with him.

Over and over he rehearsed in his head, and sometimes to his closest friends, the reasons for his father's success and his...failure? No he could never admit to that, his... lesser success.

'Dad started in the good times, and got out just when they were turning sour, and I bet he saw them coming, crafty bugger.' He would argue. 'In the fifties cars broke down, and now, for the most part they don't. In the fifties there was a decent margin on petrol, but now the big boys— the BPs, the Shells — were fast becoming mini supermarkets and squeezing down pump prices so the small independents like Willard's just couldn't compete.'

'Well', he confided to Deborah, hoping to convince himself as much as his wife, 'there's nothing for it — I've just got to match their stores with one of my own.'

Yes, it was a gamble, and an expensive one, but what else could he do?

He had no qualifications. He had learned his trade on the job.

The garage wasn't just his livelihood it was his life.

He talked the problem over and over with Deborah until the strain told on both of them. It was time to be decisive.

So one evening at supper he said 'Debbie!' in a tone that made her stop eating and look up.

'Debbie,' he repeated, "I have made up my mind, about the business.'

Her heart sank, like a prisoner in the dock she could guess the verdict from his tone.

Ian took a deep breath. 'I'm going ahead with the expansion plans.'

She waited for him to finish, but it seemed he had.

'OK.' she said.

'OK? Just OK?'

'What more is there to say. You know I'm not happy about the idea, but that damn garage has been our life for so long, I can't think what we'd do without it. I'm behind you all the way.'

Ian beamed with pleasure. What a woman! He got up, went round the table and gave his wife a huge bear hug. 'Don't be daft.' she said but hugged him back.

'There are only two small hurdles,' he said, arms still round Deborah.

'We haven't got the money?' she suggested.

'OK, there are only three small hurdles.'

The old joke lightened their mood, and he sat down again.

'Yes, you're right. One, we haven't got the money. Two, we haven't got planning permission. Yet.'

'Yet?'

'I've been feeling out the mood in the council offices. Basically, with local elections due next Spring they're very keen to be seen helping local businesses. We're a high profile business right on the main road, if we went bust the whole world would soon know about it. So...well, fingers crossed.'

'And the money?'

'Ah, the money.'

'How much do you need? Do we need, I mean'

'That's my girl. All told, about £50- 60,000.'

'Can the business afford it?'

'No. We'll have to borrow from the bank.'

'But will they lend?' She knew the Banks were hoarding their cash since the so-called credit crunch.

'They've made very good money out of Willard's over the years, they can bloody well pay some of it back.' he blustered, before adding with less certainty, 'well, we'll see. I think I've got a good proposition. And they'll want some kind of collateral, no doubt.'

'Collateral? Is that some kind of guarantee?'

'Yes. It could be the business,' he hesitated before adding, 'it could be the house.'

'This house?' the alarm in her eyes made him flinch. 'Do you mean that if you couldn't pay off the loan, they'd take this house? Oh Ian!'

'Don't worry, darling, it won't come to that.'

She studied him intensely.

He never called her darling. It didn't reassure her.

While Brian's company was drawing up the plans, Ian wrote a business plan for the new improved Willard's. As soon as the drawings were ready he would present the complete package to the Bank.

Until then it was business as usual. He picked up the 'phone in his cramped office by the showroom and punched in a number.

'Hello, Marcus Strickland.'

'Marcus, It's Ian Willard. Do you remember telling me about some old wreck in your stables? Is it still there?'

Marcus laughed. 'It's not going anywhere, it has no wheels. I was thinking of asking the council to come and take it away.'

Ian made a silent grimace. Another wasted journey, by the sound of it — but at least a short one.

'You mind if I come and have a look at it, sometime.'

'Delighted, old boy. Today suit you?'

'Today's fine. About eleven?'

'Make it twelve,' Marcus said, 'and we can have a glass of wine, when you've seen it.' Marcus was very partial to a glass of wine.

'Twelve it is.'

'Stables' does scant justice to the handsome listed building where once the master's proud horses were pampered and petted by a dozen altogether less privileged coachmen, grooms and stable lads.

The mellowed red brick frontage boasts an elegant clock tower and the Georgian sash windows of the accommodation above the stables all add to the impression of reassuring prosperity. Tall wide doors open onto a substantial interior, now a parking lot for the tenant farmer's tractors, lorry and old Land Rovers, but once housing those much prized steeds and the elegant carriages they pulled to glittering balls across the county.

Marcus led Ian to the two remaining stalls, where two chestnut mares were lazily munching hay.

'Good girl, Lightning.' He patted one of them which nuzzled his hand, looking for sugar. 'And you, Thunder.' More patting before he turned to Ian. 'You ride, do you old boy?' How easily the privileged can make you feel less so.

'Only cars.'

'Hmmpf. Noisy, smelly things. Now, on a mare like this galloping over the soft turf...what car can give you a feeling like that?'

Marcus had been Master of the local hunt. How he missed those exhilarating gallops and daring jumps as he raced ahead of the field on his favourite stallion.

'I was anticipating rather more than two horse power.' Ian interrupted the older man's day dream.

'Yes, yes, let's go and look at the old jalopy.'

There were several store rooms at the back. and tucked away in the corner of the furthest and darkest one and hidden under an old torn dust sheet was the car.

But first they had to remove a great pile of scaffolding boards and ladders and old boxes that barred the way.

'Bit of a mess I'm afraid. I haven't been in here for years.' Marcus wriggled to the front of the dust sheet. 'Let's get this off.' And he started to pull at his end of the sheet.

Ian took the other and they lifted off the sheet, sending a cloud of dust spinning into the air.

'Well there it is. Sorry Ian, but I did tell you it was an old wreck.'

MAY THE BEST MAN WIN

The Times is propped against the coffee pot, and as Brian reads he idly spoons muesli into a bowl and trails his cuff in the butter. Marcia is opening the post, a pale February sun painting hazy patterns on the polished oak table.

It's a Saturday morning after a tedious dinner party that had stumbled on past one o'clock and the Woodrows are consoling themselves with a long, lazy, late brunch.

'Oh Good!' Marcia waves an invitation at Brian, 'Helena and Jasper have finally fixed their wedding day.' Helena Willard is Brian's God daughter and special favourite of the childless Woodrows. Our virtual daughter, Brian calls her.

'About time, too,' he says now, 'but no, that's great news. Where is the wedding?'

'The Church of the Holy Rude in Stirling.' Marcia reads

'Stirling? In Scotland?' Brian sounds peeved. 'What's wrong with Winchcombe?'

'I rather fancy the McCabes are footing the bill. Helena tells me they are very big wigs up near Callander. Lairds or something.'

She studies a letter that came with the invitation. 'It all looks rather grand.'

'Go on.'

Marcia reads, 'Dress code: Tailcoats, top hats, posh frocks - and of course a stunning hat for me.'

'Oh God. Another trip to Moss Bros.'

'They've reserved 40 rooms for wedding guests at a hotel in Stirling.' She reads.

'Ah that's nice. We're invited to a dinner at the McCabe's the night before the wedding - black tie or kilt.'

'Oh, very posh. Black tie dinner, Tails and topper for the wedding - when is this great society event in the Scottish calendar, or should that be Callander?'

'The wedding is on Saturday 16th June at 11.00 am,' reads Marcia 'and afterwards at Callander House. The dinner's on the Friday evening, of course.' And that's when the fly flew into the ointment. Marcia would have flicked it out with a minimum of effort, but Brian prods and pokes at it until it was well and truly stuck fast.

'June 16th? I've a nasty feeling that's the Captains' Day lunch.'

He hurries from the room, and returns with his diary. 'Oh bugger! It *is* June 16th, and there's a special dinner the night before. We have a problem.'

'No we don't, Brian. You can't possibly miss your god daughter's wedding — just for a lunch at the golf club.' Marcia's tone suggests there's little room for compromise.

'It isn't 'just a lunch at the golf club,' Brian mimicking Marcia, ' I've told you before, it's the day the captain's of all the Gloucestershire clubs - and their *wives*' he adds, glaring at Marcia 'get together for an annual celebration and this year we're the hosts. Black tie dinner on the Friday - now there's a coincidence - a match and lunch on the Saturday.'

Marcia doesn't respond.

'Well Marcia?...so?' A bit aggressive, now.

'So what?'

'You don't see just the tiniest little difficulty, here?'

'Only if you are determined to make it one, which it looks like you are.'

'As club Vice Captain, and Captain-elect, you may remember —'

'How can I forget!'

'—it's my job, my *privilege*, to formally welcome all the other captains at the dinner. I've already had some thoughts for my speech.'

'Really? It's four months away!'

'Of course, if I miss the event, I might not be elected Captain at the AGM.'

Marcia says nothing. She would be delighted if Brian wasn't elected. She's pretty sure he will lose patience with all the demands on the Club Captain, once the kudos of having his own parking place and receiving the 'New Captain's Jacket' has worn off. She has already told him that she refuses to play the loyal, ever present wife.

'But you could go to Scotland without me,' he says, without conviction.

'And what shall I tell Helena on the happiest day of her life? That the Godfather she dotes on was unable to be at her wedding because he was swiping at a little white ball with a stick?'

'OK, OK. Let's leave it. I'll try and think of a solution.' He notices the butter on his dressing gown and tries to wipe it off with a tissue. It just smears. 'Bugger.' Brian is out of sorts.

He couldn't, of course, think of a solution, and it would be too painful to relate a blow-by-blow account of the subsequent discussions that the reader will recognise could only have one outcome. Andy Grice, a past captain, would deputise for Brian at the Golf Club — a decision the committee agreed a little too readily, Brian thought. And Brian would go to the wedding, a victory Marcia suspected would have to be paid for with a very grumpy husband.

But as the wedding approached the grumpiness evaporated. Two days in a beautiful part of Scotland, to see his lovely Helena married, and himself released from the obligation to concoct and deliver a witty speech at the club...the appeal of the trip grew by the day. Helena had described the McCabe's house as 'an absolute mansion, uncle Brian,' with thousands of acres, including two Munros. And deer in the park and a river with half a mile of salmon fishing rights.

'And what's a Munro?' Brian asked.

'It's a mountain that's more than 3,000 feet high. There are almost 300 in Scotland. Some people climb them all.'

'Hmmm. What kind of masochist does that?'

'Well, Jasper does for a start!' Helena, says defensive and proud. 'He's climbed over a hundred and his father has 'knocked off', as they say, all the lot.'

'Bully for him. Anyway the house sounds very grand, I'm looking forward to the dinner there. Will there be many people?'

'Oh, I think just close family and friends and Mummy and Daddy and you and auntie Marcia as Godparents. I think the table can only sit about 40.'

'Only 40!?' Brian is impressed despite himself. His table can sit eight or an uncomfortable ten. He had Googled the hotel in Stirling. Very promising —

solid granite walls and the towers and turrets of a small castle. Handsome bedrooms, and he was pleased to see it was someway from the road. He is easily upset by noise. And in mid-June it would be light in Scotland till well past eleven o'clock, they could stroll along the river before bed. He was less happy at the quantity of clothing that seemed to be required — the dinner suit, the tailcoat, top hat and pinstripes, the traveling clothes. Marcia, too, needed a large suitcase and a hatbox. Alan Meadows, shook his head in wonder when they piled their luggage into his mini-cab. He was to pick them up again the very next evening.

Marcia and Brian had planned everything with care to make this short visit a success, except square off Al Qaeda.

They had allowed ample time to get to Heathrow, they had hired a car to drive from Edinburgh to Callender for the dinner, paid too much (Brian thought) for the best room in the hotel, and spent too much (Brian again thought) on Helena and Jasper's wedding present. Bought the hat, the shoes and a dress for her, hired the tails, top hat and bought new shoes, new shirt and white tie, for him.

'This wedding,' Brian grumbled, 'is costing more than a long weekend in Rome.'

'You're such a skinflint. This is your God daughter for Goodness sake. I knew you'd be like this.'

'Like what?'

'Like this. Grumbling at every turn just because you missed your precious golf.'

'I knew you'd be like this,' he said.

'Like what?' Marcia laughed.

'Like this. Coiled, ready to accuse me of sulking if I make the tiniest criticism. Well, I intend to enjoy every last minute.'

The cab was hopping between motorways on the A404 when Alan Meadows tentatively asked if he could get the one o'clock headlines. He knew the Woodrows preferred to drive in silence, but he badly wanted to catch the lunchtime Test score. He never did.

'If you must,' Brian says grudgingly. Alan pushes a button and Brian checks his watch against the time signal. 'Pip - pip - pip - pip - pip - piiip'

'The news at one o clock. A terrorist alert has closed Heathrow airport. All outgoing flights have been cancelled, all incoming flights are being diverted. At 10 o'clock this morning the security services intercepted a message that convinced the authorities that the airport is under serious threat.'

'OH SHIT!' wails Brian.

'Ssh! Listen.' urges Marcia.

'....indication, yet, when the airport will re-open. A spokesman for BAA says that it will be several hours at least, and perhaps longer. Gatwick, Luton and Stanstead are open though long delays are likely as Heathrow flights are being diverted there. Passengers for domestic flights are advised to call Flight information for details.'

The story was then repeated at greater length.

Alan Meadows pulls the car into a lay-by and waits for instructions. Silence. Not even Brian swearing. Blank looks, empty minds. Then they creak into action. Slow, then gathering pace. Both Marcia's and Brian's and once or twice Alan's mobile phone are pressed into service. Cars and lorries and coaches hurtle past whipping the thin trees into frantic motion, and they gaze unseeing across the green spring fields and plead and plan with a dozen unhelpful and obliging, patient and indifferent voices.

And little by little a solution of sorts is reached. Far from ideal - but a solution. After many false starts, they have finally procured the two last seats on Easyjet's 19.45hrs flight from Stansted to Glasgow. It is due to arrive at nine o'clock. They have cancelled the car hire at Edinburgh and rebooked it for Glasgow. They have called the hotel, and they have spoken to someone at Callander House (all the McCabes out at a wedding rehearsal) who took a message but offered no advice. It's about an hour's drive Brian calculates from the airport to Callander, so if they left the airport at 9.20pm, say, they would arrive at about 10.15pm. Their dinner invitation, embossed gold on thick white card, said '7.30pm for eight o' clock. Black Tie or Kilt.'

Brian suggests they could join the party for the pudding and a drink, but Marcia scoffs at the idea.

'It's a formal dinner with people we don't know, and if we don't go to the hotel in Stirling first how can we possibly put on our dinner clothes. I'm certainly not changing in a lay-by like this.'

'Surely, they'd appreciate us making an effort?' Brian knows he's clutching at straws, but is reluctant to admit it. In the event the decision is made for them — by the baggage handlers at Stansted airport, overwhelmed by the surge of extra passengers, by the air traffic controllers at Glasgow coping with the ripples of disruption from Heathrow, and by the sole girl at the airport car-hire desk faced with a sudden stampede of tired and impatient customers. It's 11 o'clock when they drive from Glasgow airport. And after midnight when they get to the hotel in Stirling. The kitchen is shut, and their mini-bar produces a tin of nuts two packets of crisps and a chocolate bar, which feast they wash down with the half bottle of wine in the door.

Their room is huge and impersonal, with windows looking over the garden on one side, the car park on the other. It doesn't fulfil the promise of the website, but, as Brian should know more than most, that is the skill of the website designer. Far more alarming, as Brian discovers all too clearly, their room is immediately above the bar where a large group of Jasper's friends are shattering the silence with raucous shouts and huge gusts of laughter. And they show no signs of letting up as a tired Brian and Marcia crawl into bed. Finally some bagpipes are produced and the hideous wailing drowns out even the shouting and bursts of hilarity.

'Jesus Christ, that's the last straw!' Brian switches on his bedside light, and gets out of bed.

'What are you doing?'

'It's...' he picks up his watch '.. half-past one.' He pulls his coat over his pyjamas and goes out to protest.

'They're going to keep the noise down.' Brian says hopefully when he returns. And the bagpipes do stop, but soon the singing starts. Finally, at 3.00 am the party below them breaks up, and Brian is able to drift off into a troubled sleep. Marcia has been asleep for some time.

'They're just enjoying themselves, don't let it bother you so much,' she had said.

A fine drizzle is falling from a grey sky onto the grey streets of Stirling when Brian pulls back the curtains a few hours later. He flicks on the television and learns that Heathrow is slowly getting back to normal but delays must be expected. Then a cheerful weather girl warns them to expect plenty of rain in Central Scotland. Poor Helena. In Gloucestershire, he notes, it will be a warm and sunny day for the golf. Well of course it will.

Brian and Marcia, she in her new hat and dress, he in tailcoat, top hat and pinstripe trousers huddle under her small umbrella as they wait in a long line to enter the church. The wet wind fusses round their legs and dampens their shoes and their spirits. The friends of the groom outnumber the friends of the bride by 10 to one, and have spilled over to the wrong side.

Brian and Marcia are ushered to a side pew near the back, before Ian Willard hurries over to lead them to reserved seats at the front. Marcia sheds a tear when Helena makes her vows. Brian takes sidelong looks at Jasper's family. Jasper's tall lean father, just built for bounding up the mountains and Jasper's two even taller brothers all impressive in their Kilts, sporrans and ceremonial jackets, and dwarfing their tiny mother in her enormous hat.

'How has that mouse produced those giants?' Brian wonders? The other women in the front pews - sisters? wives? girlfriends?- carry an air of elegant self importance. No doubt these boys were bawling below him last night. The church is dotted with other likely suspects, tall young men in kilts, tall young women in hats.

He had always thought of the Scots as wee. Wee Scots. No doubt they were the undernourished cottagers, driven into The Highlands by the belligerent ancestors of these towering Anglo-Scots now bellowing the hymns under the shadow of the castle which had protected them over the centuries.

Most of the women are as tall as he is - taller some of them. He stands up straighter. He sings louder, and Marcia steals a glance at him. She knows her husband all too well, senses that he is already forming a lively prejudice against Helena's in-laws. Brian searches around for Helena's friends.

He recognizes very few. Helena's brother Bertram — they nod to each other — and his very plump wife Veronica, and a couple of Helena's college friends. He sourly inspects the Order of Service -- more readings, more hymns more platitudes from the vicar a benediction... on and on.

Then the bells are peeling and Jasper and Helena are walking down the aisle nodding and smiling to left and right, followed by the McCabes and the Willards, and then a general scrum, pushing politely but firmly towards the exit to get to their cars before they are gridlocked in. 'Now for the Champagne,' dreams Brian as they shuffle out of the church , 'and some proper food.'

The field set aside for the cars is a quagmire by the time Brian and Marcia arrive at Callander House. Powerful 4x4s have left deep ruts in the wet slippery grass, and the guests are picking their way through the mud towards the giant marquee. Some have brought boots for the 250 yard stretch — how did they know?, Brian wonders — a few young brutes are piggy-backing their women, but most of the guests are watching their pretty new shoes or their patent leather pumps being ruined with every step.

The roar of 400 voices in the huge tented marquee is supplemented by a group of three bagpipers. Brian winces at Marcia and grabs a glass of champagne, and soon after another as they queue to greet the bride and groom, the McCabes, the Willards and god knows who else, all standing in a smiling line.

'You missed a rare treat last night, Brian.' Ian and Deborah, Brian and Marcia are huddled together near a heater, hastily requisitioned from the barn but fighting a losing battle against the unexpected chill of the dreary June day.

'That's what the terrorists wanted,' says Marcia, 'to deprive Brian of his filthy capitalist meal.'

'Go and have a look at the house, if you have the chance. It's a ruddy palace! My daughter has done rather well for herself.'

'*His* daughter.' Deborah scoffs. 'Nothing to do with me, of course.'

'Dom Perignon to start,' Ian will not be diverted from taunting his friend, 'then Meursault Les Perrieres, followed by an '82 Chateau Palmer, and washed down with a special brandy. All served by two uniformed flunkeys. I believe the food was pretty good, too.'

'Uniformed flunkeys! They wore black jackets and white aprons.' Deborah tells Marcia.

'You're making me hungry,' Brian says, 'and thirsty'. He takes another glass of champagne from a passing waiter. He's feeling better.

'There's wine on the tables, Brian.' Marcia looks doubtfully at the already half empty champagne glass. His fourth glass? His fifth?

The speeches are endless. A professional photographer and a film maker are capturing every action, every word as one young man after another recalls, amongst great hilarity, episodes of Jasper's life, that he had spent years trying to forget. Helena sits tense and gamely smiling at the long raised table for the wedding party. Her father had made some very loving and witty remarks about her, and everybody clapped. But that was half an hour ago. Since then it had been Jasper, Jasper, Jasper. Brian pours himself another glass of red wine and the anger mounts. This whole ruddy wedding is for the glorification of the bloody McCabes. Their great house, their matchless history, their mighty exploits, the assumption of superiority.

Unbearable. Helena, his sweet and lovely God daughter, it occurs to Brian, was no more than a supporting actor in this ghastly Scottish swanking.

'Bloody shame!' he mutters.

'I beg your pardon?' The lady on his right is looking at him sharply.

She had scarcely acknowledged Brian to that point, nor had anyone else on their table after the initial introductions. But she had noticed Brian repeatedly filling his glass, and had not hidden her disapproval.

'If I hear anymore about Jasper's university binges, his cars, his girlfriends or his horses, I shall throw up.' Brian is doing his best to upset this sour looking woman.

'I daresay you will!' She looks pointedly at his glass, 'I just pray you don't do it anywhere near me.' She turns scornfully way from Brian, and whispers to her neighbour on the other side, who looks over at Brian with ill-feigned dislike.

Brian needs a pee. Quite suddenly and quite badly. He means to wait for a pause in the speeches, but he can't. He gets up a little unsteadily and squeezes through the tables bumping into some of them apologetically, and makes for an exit which isn't. He finds himself in the caterers tent, bustling and clattering. He stumbles through the tent flap at the back and into a field. At last the rain has stopped, and a pale sun lightens the canvas of the marquee, but where are the promised portable lavatories? He starts to walk round the marquee, but his need is great, and then he is peeing against the side of it. From inside the marquee another shout of laughter and then a great cheer. Another good joke at Jasper's expense, no doubt. He zips up his flies and wanders round the marquee to the entrance. As he walks into the marquee another great cheer goes up, but not for Jasper, everybody in the marquee is looking and laughing at Brian.

They don't stay much longer. Helena appears particularly embarrassed that her grand new family and their smug friends have all witnessed her Godfather silhouetted so starkly against the tent and relieving himself. Jasper tries hard not to smirk, but his friends are openly gleeful. Jasper's father says goodbye and shakes Brian's hand but he doesn't smile. They walk to their car through the mud, and Marcia takes the key from Brian and drives them back to Glasgow airport. They have a long wait. They are very early for their flight which in turn is very late. They change out of their wedding clothes in the toilet. Brian has a thumping headache. Marcia doesn't refer to the 'incident' until they are on the plane, high above the dark grey clouds weeping still on a soggy Scotland. Brian gets up to go for a pee.

'Try not to do it on the outside of the plane, Brian.' She says sweetly.

GETTING THE MESSAGE

High above the Atlantic, high above the clouds high above the Atlantic, Derek Henderson finally plucked up the courage to show his round-robin letter to his wife.

That he had to steel himself to do so suggests that he was far from confident of Ursula's reaction, and that had he shown her earlier she might have ridiculed the idea, and even talked him out of it.

If only she had!

Already the bravado with which he'd sent it, just 24 hours earlier, was waning.

Was it such a clever idea to invite his friends to put him under the microscope? And why on earth had he kept the idea from his wife?

Ever since he had met Ursula at one of Quentin Moore's distinctly odd birthday parties — this time his 27th and a half — Derek Henderson had harboured a nagging feeling that he had never quite earned her respect and admiration.

Perhaps because he had made such an inauspicious start.

He had arrived at the party to be thrown into a room of total strangers — and worse, just the kind of strangers whom he most disparaged, or perhaps suspected disparaged him.

They communicated in a sluggish Eton drawl punctuated by high-pitched whinnies of mirth. They had lots of 'chums', wealth but nothing as vulgar as money, and no obvious means of attaining it, except from 'pater' or 'The Trust'.

Hanging on their arms and every word were leggy Melindas and Jacindas apparently in thrall to their braying jokes and unshakeably cocky opinions.

Even so, had they as much as acknowledged his existence, nodded at his stories, smiled perhaps at his jokes, he might have found them 'not a bad bunch, when you got to know them.'

But they didn't acknowledge his existence, let alone nod at his stories or laugh at his jokes.

And Derek's prejudice, so speedily formed, was fuelled by every back turned to him, every conversation that pointedly excluded him.

In such a hostile environment it is perhaps forgivable that he reached for the bottle for a little dutch courage — enough, indeed, to fill a small Amsterdam canal.

Ursula had been placed next to him at supper, but after a friendly 'Hello I'm Ursula,' had reverted to talking and laughing with friends across the table.

His attempt to join in the banter were studiously ignored, and he was reduced once again to an angry spectator of their imbecilic cackling at their own clumsy, self-satisfied wit.

Such inconsiderate behaviour is not rare in the young — Derek Henderson, himself, was not blameless — but it had angered him a great deal more than it should have done, and certainly didn't justify his response.

If it was the wine that had aggravated his sense of rejection then his solution of increasing his intake was not perhaps the wisest one.

Several glasses later he started to tell a story in a loud and grating voice. No matter that no one at the table was listening, he was determined to be as obnoxious to this 'gaggle of brainless upper class fools' as they had been to him.

So he just talked on in this harsh, penetrating monotone until eventually all the table was watching him with various degrees of amazement or disdain.

Still Derek didn't stop. He continued to bark out a stream of nonsense as the anger around him mounted.

'What the hell is the man on about?!'

'What's the man *on*, more like.'

'The man's as pissed as a newt.'

'For God's sake, man, DO SHUT UP!'

'Man' was clearly not a compliment.

Now that he had the table's undivided attention, Derek laughed unpleasantly.

'Boring isn't it? Having to listen to a stream of utter fucking rubbish.' Derek glared round the table. 'For an hour and a half I've had to endure your witless, arrogant nonsense. One more fucking syllable and I'll go stark, staring mad.'

And with an unsteady flourish he rose and no doubt would have flounced triumphantly from the table and Quentin Moore's idiotic party had he not stumbled, caught his foot on Ursula's chair and crashed in a heap on the floor, taking Ursula down with him.

There was a great gust of laughter from the table above them, which Ursula tangled up on the floor beside him joined in, before asking him, not unkindly, if he was alright.

'Oh Piss off, you silly bitch,' he had replied, before rising with difficulty and staggering out of the room.

It took Derek three weeks to find the courage to call Quentin Moore and get Ursula's address and another two weeks to write the apology to Ursula herself.

She had replied by return, laughing off the whole incident, and apologising if they had 'rather overlooked him' at the party, explaining that as old friends who hadn't met for some time they had got rather carried away catching up.

She added a vague invitation to come over to the flat she shared with three other girls for a drink sometime and signed it, Love Ursula.

Ursula signed all her letters in the same affectionate manner, but Derek wasn't to know that, and thus encouraged he did indeed take up her invitation to a drink, and found that the girl he had wrestled to the floor was not only tremendous fun, but was also the daughter of an 'Honourable' and a 'Lady', grand daughter of an Earl, and heir with two siblings to a considerable Estate. She was also quite pretty - 'OK, not a 10/10 stunner, maybe, but certainly a seven and a half or maybe even an eight,' as he told his friends.

And since most people, consciously or not, pair off with someone of similar physical appeal, that probably meant that Ursula rated his looks as a 'seven and a half out of ten or maybe even an eight.' Lower, it must be said, than he rated himself.

Now he handed his open letter to Ursula on the 747 with some of the same trepidation with which he had sent the first all those years ago.

'What's this?' She looked at the envelope with some surprise.

'Read it.' he said, and watched rather nervously as she did.

When she arrived at the last paragraph which asked for replies on their return from The Galapagos she reacted for the first time.

'My goodness, what an... intrepid... I might think of a better word later...what an intrepid husband I have. Did you actually send it.'

'Yes, of course I did,' he said with more bravado than he felt 'an interesting idea, don't you think?'

'Who to? Who did you send it to?'

'Our friends, the people I work with,' then added hesitantly ...'some of the family.'

'Not our children?!'

Peter aged eight, and Jade nine were playing a noisy game of SNAP! in the seats behind them.

'No, no. of course not. But I still think-----'

'Mummy and Daddy?'

'I didn't send one to your mother, no.'

'But you sent one to Daddy?'

'Yes, I did. I thought it would be instructive to know how he sees the man who married his daughter.' 'Oh, Derek, how could you? You know how he frets over the slightest thing these days. He'll work himself up into a complete lather about it. I better call him from Quito and tell him it was just a joke and to ignore it.'

'Now, hold on a minute, Ursula. The whole point is to get a range of opinions from a varied group of people. You might as well ring up everyone else and tell them to ignore it.'

If only she would.

They sat in silence for a while, till he blurted out 'You don't seem to approve of the idea of the letter.'

'It doesn't bother me one way or the other. I just don't want it to bother my family. I expect our friends will probably make light of it. Though some may even take it seriously, I suppose.' Then after a moment she added, 'Will you show me their replies?'

'Aha! You want to see them, then?'

'Yes, of course.'

'So you do find the letter quite intriguing?' There was a hint of pleading in his voice.

'I'm intrigued that you felt the need to send it.'

She turned back to her book, but almost at once asked for the letter back.

He gave it to her, but when she said ,'I suppose I'd better answer it', he grabbed the letter out of her hands.

'Don't be silly, darling, I wouldn't dream of sending one to you.'

'Why on earth not. Isn't your wife's opinion important? Or perhaps you think you know it, already?'

'Of course, it's important. And yes, I think I have a pretty good idea what you think of me. Haven't I?'

'You'll have to wait and see.'

'I shan't read it, if you do. I would be devastated if you said anything critical. I'd rather believe you think the world of me. Just as I think the world of you, of course.'

'Of course.'

It must be said that Derek Henderson did not get the unalloyed pleasure he had hoped for from the marine iguanas of the Galapagos Islands or Machu Pichu or Cotopaxi volcano in Ecuador, That bloody letter was hanging over him like the cloud that so often hung over the volcano. Even before he had opened a single reply he had, indeed, learned one insight about himself. He was a damned idiot.

It was a damp, chilly morning when Derek and Ursula paid off the taxi and lugged their suitcases and bags into the hall of their 'Prestige Gated Residence'.

While the children rushed to their sorely missed computer games, Ursula checked that the plants had been watered properly, then put on a kettle.

By the time it was boiling Derek had already gathered up all the mail and was sorting it into piles.

First his pile and then Ursula's pile.

Then he subdivided his. Junk mail. Official letters with cellophane windows. Large, thick envelopes from regular suppliers or Companies. Typed smaller envelopes, including two, he noticed, from his office. Hand written envelopes, which he carefully put aside.

Those, he imagined, would be in response to his round robin.

There were just 14 of them.

Derek was both disappointed and relieved - but, on balance, mostly the latter.

Such a modest response would suggest a considerable indifference to his 'interesting idea', or maybe to him.

On the other hand, since he had first asked everyone to dispassionately dissect him he had quite decided that was the last thing he wanted.

He stared at the envelopes, trying to guess whose writing it was, while Ursula leaned on the door jamb drinking her tea.

'Go on then,' she urged, 'get the good news.'

'Or the not so good news.' He hesitated, shuffling the letters through his hands. 'No, I'm too tired at the moment.'

'Coward.' Ursula laughed, but she turned away to fiddle with the central heating control.

Derek started to go through his other piles. Junk mail straight to the bin. He glanced briefly at the larger, heavier envelopes, some could wait, some looked more important, then he started on the 'window' mail, but after reading a bank statement (quite pleasing) and a gas bill (outrageous) he pushed the rest aside and picked up the small typed letters.

He ripped open one with 'The Gloucester Daily Times' stamped on the envelope.

The Gloucester Daily Times

5th October 2011

Dear Mr Henderson

Welcome back from The Galapegos. Perhaps you do not know, but while you were there your round robin letter was printed in our paper. A copy came to our notice and we thought the 'idea' might be of interest to our readers, and as it was an open letter, we felt at liberty to publish it.

It did, indeed, provoke a response. Not all of it positive I am afraid, and we would like to offer you the opportunity to answer your critics. We would like, anyway, to arrange an interview, to learn more about you and why you decided to write the letter, and what response you had to it.

I will ring you in a few days, after you have re-acclimatized to Gloucester life.

Yours sincerely
Penelope Draper

'Not all of it positive, I am afraid.' Derek sighed and glanced at the letters he had separated from the rest. What would he find in them? Nothing but negatives, criticism and ridicule?

He pulled the letters toward him and started reading.

When he had put down the last one he sat gazing out at his soggy English garden, the first wet leaves on the lawn, the jacuzzi pool shut down and covered up for the dreary winter ahead.

What did he feel? Deflated? Was that the word he wondered? No, flat. That was the word.

Derek Henderson felt as flat as his big idea had fallen.

The negatives, criticism or ridicule did not materialise - except in the mildest manner.

Which was a relief.

But nor did the insights, the great positives, the strong affections or admiration.

Most of the writers seemed anxious neither to upset his feelings, nor boost his ego.

The general tenor of the messages blandly reassured him that he was good company, could be funny at times, and stubborn at others, that if he had skeletons in the cupboard, the writer wasn't aware of them, and that they hoped to enjoy his and Ursula's company for years to come.

But from 66 of the recipients - nothing.

Then he started on the rest of his mail. He opened the two from his office, smiled when he read the Chief clerk's letter 'what a pompous ass' and frowned when he read Macklin's. 'What a pompous ass' he thought again — but this time with some misgiving. Had one of his client's really taken such offence at the letter? Or was Macklin exaggerating. His relationship with the Senior Partner was businesslike, but there was little warmth between them. In the early days he had made an effort to be friendly with his superior —partly for the sake of his career, partly to create a more pleasant atmosphere in the building, but Macklin had seen Derek's friendliness as familiarity and not encouraged it. No doubt he saw the letter as further evidence of his younger partner's naivety.

Oh dear, now he would have to placate the old fool. Tomorrow he would assess the situation and worm his way back into his partners' good books. He was confident he could do that.

But that confidence was dented when he discovered a letter hidden between two Company reports.

It did not make happy reading.

> 'Henderson - I cannot bring myself to prefix your name with 'Dear' even as a meaningless convention.
>
> I read your arrogant self-important letter with growing bile. God knows why you sent it to me. Even an insensitive thick-skinned bastard like you must have sensed my antipathy towards you. But clearly you have not.'

Derek glanced to the bottom of the page. The letter was not signed. No surprise there.

> 'It is a source of real distaste to me that as we share so many common acquaintances I have often to endure your company. Short of refusing all invitations where there is any chance you might also appear, or of not going to a theatre, cinema or restaurant where I might meet you,

there is little I can do to avoid your obnoxious company.

Since you ask for a totally honest assessment I will endeavour to give you mine.

First of all I know nobody who would be so vainglorious as to send such a letter in the first place - except you. I know nobody so stupid to send such a letter - except you. Every gesture you ever make, every laboured joke, every self-glorifying story shouts 'look at me — look what a grand fellow I am.' You are trivial, shallow, cocky, boring...

It's no use, I am working myself up into a lather, just thinking about you. And I refuse to let such a loathsome little man as you upset me.

I will not sign this letter. I do not wish you to know which of your so-called 'friends' detests you so much. I will not divulge my sex. But I doubt if I am the only one of either sex who finds you so repulsive.

And don't hope to discover the writer in the style of the writing. That too is disguised. But before you dismiss this as the work of some bitter crank who saw your letter in The Gloucester Daily Times, I will tell you something that no stranger would know. At The Porters' carol party last December I saw you drop a soggy canapé on the carpet and walk quickly away as though it wasn't you. How bloody typical.

No, Henderson, I am not a stranger — I have no doubt that you would be very surprised and maybe even shocked to learn my identity. May you rot in hell!'

Derek put the letter down. Then he picked the letter up and re-read it. Then he put it under a pile of the other letters and gazed vacantly out of the window.

He didn't have to know the writer's identity to be 'very surprised and even shocked'. He was completely taken aback by the ferocity of the attack as it was.

The canapé. Yes, he remembered dropping the canapé on the carpet, and not stopping to pick it up as he usually would.

But somebody had seen him. Somebody who had been watching him with hate-filled eyes.

Who? That is the question that will haunt him for months. Who?

The letter and the envelope had been printed from a computer, was postmarked Cheltenham and dated 28th September. It could be anybody. But who?

No, not anybody. Someone at The Porters' carol party. How many? Sixty? Seventy?

Would they still have a list? Would it help? Or just make him paranoid?

Yes he was getting paranoid. Just forget it. Was it a joke? Would one of his friends own up to it with a laugh. 'Bet it gave you a bit of a wobbly moment, Derek, admit it.'

And if not that, did it matter that one of his 'friends' didn't like him?

Well, hated, despised. loathed him. Best thing was just to forget it, not much he could do about it anyway.

Of course he couldn't just forget it.

Who?

Someone he should have sensed an antipathy from. But he hadn't. He rather prided himself on his ability to rub along well with just about anybody.

Who?

He had not treated Viv Ward terribly well all those years ago — but they had long since made up. Surely she couldn't still be bearing such a deep grudge against him, could she?

Who?

He'd made a pass at Greta once which upset her — he had limped around with a badly bruised foot for days (he had told Ursula he dropped a case of wine onto it), but hers was one of the 14 replies he had received. So he could rule her out, couldn't he?

Who?

Names, faces scrolled endlessly through his head, but none seemed plausible writers of so virulent a letter. Who had been at the Porter's party? The same faces, same names, same dead end.

He would show the letter to Ursula — perhaps she could guess at his secret despiser.

But then he prevaricated. Would she just laugh it off, tell him he's asked for it?

Probably.

But he did show the letter to Ursula, and she did laugh it off and she did tell him he'd asked for it. All the same he did feel better for sharing the spiteful missive. Perhaps he should share it with others, too. There was a dinner at Ben and Judith Cox's house on Friday, he could read it to all of them there.

No he couldn't. For one thing he had no idea who else was going - suppose the person who wrote it was there, hiding behind a false smile, revelling in his discomfort. For another the prospect of reading out a litany of all his perceived vileness didn't appeal.

No, he would just lock the damn thing away in his drawer — oddly, he never thought of destroying it — and lock the disagreeable sentiments in the deepest recesses of his mind, where they couldn't bubble up and disturb his generally well established equanimity, not to say self-satisfaction.

Easier said than done.

From the day that he had received that poisonous letter on their return from The Galapagos, Derek Henderson was never in the company of any of the people to whom he had sent his round-robin letter, without a nagging and persistent feeling that one of them might have sent the offensive reply.

He was more guarded, more wary, more observant, searching for antipathies that were not there. Wondering, wondering, wondering.

'Derek seemed out of sorts,' Jim Ward slurred his words slightly despite a determined effort not to, as Viv drove him back from a lunch at the Henderson's, 'I've never known him so bloody shubdued.'

'Yes I thought so, too,' she said, 'he's not usually backward in coming forward.'

Jim stifled a hiccough, but not quite, by asking 'Did you reply to that letter he sent?'

'No. I was going to, and I did get as far as beginning to make a list of all his good and bad points. But I never sent a reply. I'm glad I didn't, now. Did you?'

But Jim was already asleep.

'You were quiet, today.' Ursula was washing the crystal wine glasses that were too precious to go into the machine.

Derek proved her point by not replying.

'You OK, sausage? Not unwell? Worried about work?'

'I'm fine.'

'I don't remember you telling a single joke.'

No reply.

'That's serious. Not a single joke.'

'Look I wasn't feeling humorous, OK?' then after a pause, 'as a matter of fact I was wondering —' he stopped.

'What? What were you wondering?'

'If any of those so called friends who were drinking my wine, and gorging on my food — our food — was the nasty little bugger who sent that anonymous letter to me.'

Ursula stopped washing a glass and cast a worried glance at her agitated husband, but she said nothing.

'Well? They could have been,' he urged.

Later she tried to talk him out of his growing paranoia. Tried to soothe his irrational fears. She reminded him that their guests, Jim and Viv, Brian and Marcia are four of their oldest friends, And although they had not known Michael and Marjorie Hurst as long, they had always been extremely friendly. If he started to suspect good friends like those in no time he would have no friends at all.

'And anyway,' she went on, 'whoever sent you that letter is not only a coward hiding behind her anonymity, but is clearly not mentally balanced. Probably makes a habit of sending nasty anonymous messages. Probably forgotten you, already. It really isn't worth getting worked up about, Derek. It really isn't.'

'You think it's a woman? You said 'her' anonymity. What makes you think it's a woman? Has someone confided in you?'

'Interesting. Yes, I did say 'her' didn't I? I don't know why. I really haven't been wondering who sent it, at all. Can I have another look at it? And, no, nobody has confided in me.'

Derek fetched the letter and gave it to Ursula.

When she had read it she shook her head. 'You really have got under someone's skin haven't you? But a man's or a woman's? If I had to guess I would say a woman's — but that might just be because you're a bit of a male chauvinist.'

'Only a woman would say such a damn silly thing as that.'

Ursula burst out laughing. Her husband had made a joke— which was a good sign, at least.

Derek Henderson studied his wife and wondered if he'd ever understand her. Why on earth was she laughing?

No result at Twickenham

Brian Woodrow was lying on a grassy bank and Daphne Gunn was lying naked by his side, her head cradled in his left arm, her almond eyes smiling up at him as he gently stroked her breasts.

He woke up with a start, guilty, disturbed, and yet tantalised by the vivid dream —reluctant to let it slip away into the fog where dreams evaporate. He lay in the darkness beside Marcia and wondered at this erotic surprise.

And it was a surprise. Brian was sure he had no lascivious designs on Douglas Gunn's grieving widow, but are not dreams suppressed fears and desires seeping to the surface?

Had the kindness he had shown Daphne when they dined in the cosy Cotswold pub, been no more than seduction dressed up as sympathy?

After too many long dark minutes he did try and banish the dream by concentrating on a problem that was troubling him at the office. At midnight it had kept him from sleep but now it acted as a sedative and soon Brian was dreaming once again.

He was running, but barely moving, to catch a train about to leave from a distant platform. But as he struggled across the foot bridge, lugging an enormous presentation portfolio, his way was suddenly blocked by a dense herd of bleating sheep. His agitation as the train pulled away from the platform was intense....

But when he woke, the dawn sun glancing through the curtains, the dream he remembered most vividly was Daphne Gunn and her soft naked skin.

This intimacy he had shared with Daphne in his sleep made him feel oddly close to her. Illogical, of course. In the first place she was happily unaware of it, and secondly their friendship had not developed as he might have expected or perhaps even hoped.

The day after their visit to the gastro pub, he had received a very warm note of thanks.

'You were so sympathetic and patient while I talked and talked,' she wrote, 'but it had been such a help. I slept last night for the first time without taking a sleeping pill.' She signed it 'love Daphne' with a little x beside her name. He kept the note on his desk for several days, before throwing it away. He felt he shared an emotional intimacy with Daphne that others did not, and that he might help her in her grief. A shoulder to cry on, perhaps. Yes, a shoulder to cry on – exactly that. So returning early from work one day and finding Daphne and Marcia worrying over fabric samples for Daphne's new kitchen, he was pleased where once he might have been vaguely irritated.

'Thank you for your note, Daphne,' he said.

'Thank you for being so understanding.' She turned to Marcia.

'Your husband was so sweet, he let me prattle on about Douglas for hours. Did he tell you?'

'He did say you shed a few tears.'

'I blubbed like a baby, actually. But I did feel better for it.'

'Perhaps we could repeat the experiment,' he said.

'Maybe.'

If Daphne's enthusiasm was muted Brian didn't notice.

'When's your next reading group Marcia?', he asked his wife.

'The 22nd. And everyone's coming here next time, so you had better make yourself scarce.'

'Well, there you are Daphne. Banished from my own house. Surely you wouldn't condemn me to eat alone?'

'Such an irresistible invitation.' She fished in her bag for a diary. 'The 22nd. A Thursday. I usually play tennis with Marjorie Hurst on Thursdays.'

'Oh.' Brian disappointed.

'But they're away that week. So, OK, supper would be good.'

But it wasn't good.

From the moment he picked her up, with great expectations, from her house, to the moment she strode back into it without a backward glance, he had struggled to find any echo of the closeness he had felt before — and she had, surely, too? They went to a highly rated but expensive restaurant in Cheltenham, where Brian ordered two large glasses of Chablis (£17) and hoped his chilly companion would be softened by the wine.

But Daphne had locked herself in and would not come out to play. He asked about her two children, he talked about Douglas, he even made polite enquiries about her damned new kitchen, for god's sake, but nothing was rewarded with more than the briefest polite response.

He tried to provoke a reaction by resorting to subjects he knew they disagreed about, and when that failed he struggled, like some medieval fool in cap and bells, to win a grudging smile or be thrown a bone by telling his favourite amusing stories.

He knew he told them well; his friends' laughter had shown him that, but in the middle of the very first one, he had caught Daphne suppressing a yawn.

'Sorry,' she said, 'it's been a long day.' It didn't help that the excellent food took so long to arrive, and when the waiter came to take their order for dessert, she declined. 'Do you mind if we skip pudding and coffee, Brian?' She asked. But offered none of the usual polite reasons. She was very tired, perhaps, or she had a very early start the next day... no, just 'Do you mind if we skip pudding and coffee, Brian?'

'Of course not,' and to the waiter, 'just the bill, please.'

And when it came, and Brian had glanced at it and gulped, Daphne made no attempt to reach for her purse as she had done in the pub. When they arrived back at her house, she thanked him, nicely enough, but offered no cheek to be pecked, shut the car door, shut the house door and was gone.

'My God! that was hard work Brian said aloud to the empty car. This time there was no thank-you note from Daphne Gunn. No 'love Daphne' and no little x.

So, that was that.

Whatever Brian Woodrow had looked for from Daphne Gunn, and he was not at all sure what that might be, was clearly not to be realised, so best put her out of his mind. He did of course meet her from time to time at social events, parties or dinners in the village but they seldom exchanged more than a few polite words.

He saw her in a new light, now. One that was more comforting to his self esteem. 'Certainly she looks attractive', he thought, studying her across the room at Derek and Ursula's Pimms party which had been driven indoors by a thunderstorm, ' but, I don't know ... there's something missing about her, and not just a husband'.

How very odd, then, that in such a frame of mind, he should dream of Daphne lying naked in his arms.

But whatever he felt about Daphne she remained aloof towards him. Her friendship with Marcia appeared to have suffered, too. They stopped going to Aerobics together, she came to their house much less often, and then only when he was away.

He was very surprised, therefore, when Daphne rang him two months later.

By chance he was working in his study on a web site for the very gastro pub where he and Daphne had had their first 'date'. As he organized the pictures of the dining room and the menus, his thoughts kept harping back to their visit. One of the photographs of the inglenook fireplace showed, in the foreground, the table they had sat at, where he had held her hand and she had cried.

'It's for you,' Marcia came in carrying the cordless phone, 'it's Daphne.'

'Daphne? For me?'

'Yes, Daphne. For you. Don't sound so surprised.'

'It's just ...... never mind.' he took the phone.

'Hello Daphne.'

'Don't sound so surprised.' Daphne laughed,

'Ah, you heard? I was working on a website for the Black Sheep. I was remembering our supper there when you called. A surprising coincidence, you must admit.'

'I remember it very well. Anyway ...'

Anyway, it transpired that Douglas Gunn had been sent two complimentary tickets to an England International at Twickenham. Douglas had long been a debenture holder at the ground but when the stadium had reopened after a year of improvements, and when Douglas had not renewed his debenture, the RFU had sent him two tickets for the match and complimentary refreshments in the Sports Bar as an inducement.

Daphne had boiled over at such insensitivity. She guessed that Douglas's name had almost certainly been picked out by computer, and that computers didn't read the obituaries. But, surely, someone should have checked?

She would throw them away, in disgust.

That was her first thought.

But no — they were expensive seats, she would give them to one of Douglas's old rugby mates.

That was her second thought.

Or maybe go herself.

Daphne had never felt the least desire to go to Rugby matches with Douglas when he was alive but now... perhaps she would feel a special closeness to her husband if she re-lived an occasion that had been so important to him?

But who could she persuade to take her? Duncan Webster, perhaps? But Duncan with a group of Douglas's other friends were going to Paris on the day to watch France play the All Blacks.

What about James? But James, her son, was flying to a stag party in Dublin. 'And, anyway, Mum I'm not that keen on Rugby.'

Graham Porter was even more discouraging. 'Nice idea, Daphne, but I'd rather watch paint dry. You know us Yanks. Baseball 1 - everything else 0.'

Michael Hurst couldn't make it. Nor a friend from Stow.

She had thought of Brain Woodrow, but Brian seemed intent on ignoring her lately. She didn't know what she had done to offend him, but she had felt his coolness. She had even stopped going to see Marcia as much as she would have wished. Which was a shame, she missed her. But by then she really did want to go to this rugby match, and so with some trepidation she had picked up the phone.

Brian, like James, was no rugby fanatic, but was flattered that Daphne had chosen to offer him the tickets.

'That's very kind, Daphne. But before I say yes I'll see if I can find someone to go with. Marcia certainly won't. I could try Jim Ward, or Ian Willard or...who else?...let me think...'

'Me?' Daphne said.

'You?' The surprise in his voice, made her smile.

'You don't seem too keen on that idea.'

'No, no. It's not that. I just thought you were offering them, because you couldn't use them. Er...well...yes, of course I'd be very happy to take you? When is it?'

'Saturday the 17th.'

'Hold on, let me call my diary up onto the screen....the 17th....the 17th.. he was hoping he wouldn't find another entry. He 'clicked' on the date. Golf with Ben Cox. Damn.

'The 17th, here we are' he said to Daphne 'no, nothing on that day. Twickenham would be fun.'

He could sort out Ben, later.

Daphne organised the day - with the help of Duncan Webster, who had done it so many times before.

'You need to book the Rugby special National Express Coach from Cheltenham to Twickenham stadium. Great party atmosphere, most people take beer or wine for the journey, so it can get a bit rowdy. If you like, I'll book you a table for lunch at a place near the ground where they know me quite well.'

'That would be kind, Duncan. Thank you. But will we have time for lunch?'

'Masses. The coach gets there two hours before the match. How many am I booking for?'

'Just two of us.'

'OK.' A short pause. 'Is that a man, Daphne?'

'Yes, Duncan, a man. A happily married man.'

It was cold and damp and grey as Brian and Daphne waited shivering with several other men for the coach to arrive at Cheltenham bus station. Neither spoke much, each supposed the other was regretting the decision to go.

And then, at last, here it comes, pulling into the bus station, splashing to a noisy halt in the bay. The doors wheezed open and they stepped up into the warmth of the coach, and a noisy party.

The coach had started from Worcester and already, at 9.00 in the morning, most of the men had open bottles of beer in front of them, and some were draped in England flags or sported large red and white England hats. Everybody seemed to be talking or calling to everybody else.

The giant bus pulled out into the traffic, and set out on its three and a half hour journey to Twickenham.

They picked up more fans in Gloucester and then Cirencester, and then they were splashing down the motorway, the huge wiper in front of the driver sweeping side to side, - thunk! squeak! thunk! squeak! thunk! squeak! - and a small television hanging the from ceiling playing highlights of old rugby games, which no one seemed to be watching, but whenever England scored they all cheered lustily.

Brian felt detached from this tiresome jollity, the almost childlike excitement, the anticipation of the afternoon match.

He rubbed the condensation from a small square of window, and looked out at the brown wet fields disappearing behind them. Maybe this wasn't such a good idea.

Then Daphne pulled a couple of glasses and a bottle of Macon from her bag, and set them on the little table that pulled down from the seat in front.

'Duncan suggested we might need this for the journey,' she said.

He looked at Daphne and laughed.

And then he bent down to the bag at *his* feet and pulled out a couple of glasses and a bottle of Pouilly Fume and set them on the little table in front of him.

'Snap!' he said.

That pleased them. Pleased with themselves, pleased with each other, pleased that suddenly the day didn't feel quite so colourless.

They decided to drink the Macon first, and leave the Pouilly Fume for the journey home. But an hour later when the Macon ran out, and the motorway ran on they decided they might just start on the second bottle.

When the coach pulled to a halt outside Twickenham stadium the second bottle was two thirds empty, and they were in high spirits. Daphne stumbled as she climbed down from the coach, and Brian took her arm.

'My legs are stiff, from sitting so long,' she said.

'Of course.' he said, and she punched him playfully on the arm.

They found the restaurant Duncan had booked, and it was heaving with rugby fans jostling for tables and drinks.

The waiters had given up on reservations. 'Sorry dear,' one of them said to Daphne as he hurtled past, 'on match days it's a bit of a scrum - excuse the pun.'

But after a while they saw a couple about to leave, and Brian just managed to reach the table before two enormous Irish fans in green and white scarves.

A small victory for England.

The table was tiny, and their knees bumped under it, and one or other would say 'sorry', until they gave up and left their knees touching.

The food came surprisingly quickly. Tomato soup, steak and chips, apple crumble, take it or leave it. They took it. 'Wine?' the waitress asked as she slapped the soup down in front of them.

'What d you think?' Brian asked Daphne.

'I don't mind, what do you think?'

But the waitress had darted away again, to serve another table.

'Ah. missed our chance, it seems.' Brian said.

But she was back in a trice, there was a good mark up on wine and she had strict orders to push it. 'Wine?'

'Yes a bottle of house red, please.' Brian ordered, and she was gone.

'That will be our third bottle!' Daphne said wide-eyed, but she didn't sound too upset.

'Sitting for a couple of hours in a cold open Stadium will sober us up,' he said.

The soup plates were whisked away, the steak plonked down, and they talked easily, happily, caught up in the boisterous atmosphere, their defences lowered by the wine.

He studied Daphne as she was eating her steak. His silence, his stillness made her look up.

'What?'

'Oh, I was just thinking...you know.'

'I'm not a mind reader.'

'OK, I was thinking that you're the third Daphne, I've shared a table with in the last few months,' he said.

'Go on,' she prompted.

He hesitated.

'Well there was the Daphne at The Black Sheep. She was unhappy and tearful and confiding. I felt quite...tender... towards her. Quite close.'

'I remember her.' Daphne said.

'Then there was the Daphne at The ****** ******* . She was bored and tired and ...closed. She couldn't wait to get home, to get away from her dull companion.'

Daphne made no attempt to deny it.

'I remember her, too,' she said

'And then there's the third Daphne, sitting at a cramped table in a raucous rugby restaurant, being bumped every time the waitress shoots past. And she's smiling and talking and fun and a bit squiffy —'

'I'm not! Well, perhaps I am.'

—'and she's good to be with. It even makes the thought of sitting for two hours in a cold damp stadium seem worthwhile.'

'So, the truth is out! You really don't like rugby at all do you?' She laughed.

'Since I am being honest, no, not much.'

'Well why did you come then?'

The question was left hanging in the air.

She wished she hadn't asked, he wondered what he could reply.

But an answer - any answer - was required.

'Why did I come?' he asked himself, aloud, stalling for time.

She came to his rescue. 'Because the tickets were free. You're a skinflint Brian Woodrow.'

'Yes, I'm as tight as a drum.'

'I think I must be getting a little tight, myself,' and she giggled to make the point, 'it's so cosy here, almost seems a pity to go out into the cold, again.'

The waitress slipped the bill onto their table without slackening her speed as she hurried past.

'Actually, I came because I wanted to be with you,' he blurted out.

'Well, thank you, that's a nice compliment.' But she was flustered, and he thought he had gone too far.

He looked away, and saw that more and more people were gathering up their coats and scarves, paying their bills, making for the door.

'Yes, well, I guess we better be going, ' he said to change the subject.

'I thought I must have upset you, somehow. You seemed to be avoiding me.'

He looked into her friendly almond eyes, such a contrast to the bored eyes of their last meal together. Was it just the wine making the difference?

'It was Daphne number 2,' he didn't elaborate.

'Forget her, Brian. She's a pain.'

'OK,' a pause, 'I dreamed about you not long ago.'

'Goodness! Was it a nightmare?' Her eyes shone.

'Anything but.'

'Well? Go on.'

He hesitated. 'I don't think I better. Now come on. We really must go to the ground, Daphne.' He got up and picked up the bill and the waitress appeared like magic at his side.

Daphne rose unsteadily, watching Brian intently, but she said nothing. Perhaps she would winkle the dream out of him later. Or perhaps she shouldn't try. Was it an erotic dream? That would be too embarrassing. Wouldn't it?

They left the restaurant and joined the tide of fans streaming towards the stadium.

In the cold air, the effects of the wine were magnified.

Her feet seemed to be floating, her head as well. She felt she would be carried away like a cork in this torrent of strangers. She hung onto Brian's arm, fiercely for support.

When they reached the turnstiles, Brian had to help her to find the tickets in her bag, and then support her up the many flights of concrete stairs to their seats.

Five minutes after the kick off, and with 80,000 fans roaring all around her, Daphne rested her head on Brian's shoulder and went to sleep.

The atmosphere on the coach trip back to Cheltenham was distinctly less animated than in the morning.

England had lost to Ireland 17 - 23, so there was no triumph to shout about, to sing about, to crow about. Several of the fans had finally succumbed to the beer that they had been drinking almost non-stop since breakfast and were slumped snoring into their seats. The television was switched off - scenes of England's former triumphs could never compensate for today's defeat.

Brian and Daphne were equally silent.

Daphne's headache was thump, thump, thumping in her temples and she had no pills to deal with it. She calculated that she must have drunk at least a whole bottle of wine, and probably almost a bottle and a half. She had brought the wine to help her relax, and Brian, too. She had anticipated that they might need it, to thaw their recent frosty relations.

And thinking about it, she had been right. Would the trip up, would the restaurant have been half as much fun if they had been stone cold sober?

Stone cold sober. No wonder kids were binge drinking, she thought, if sober was branded as stoney and cold.

But the wine had also blunted her reasons for going to the stadium where Douglas had spent so many happy afternoons. She had wanted to experience some of that pleasure, to see the day through Douglas' eyes.

That would have been easier if her own eyes hadn't been closed for so much of the game.

She had slept through the whole first half, and then her alcohol level topped up by the complimentary half-time drink in the Sports Bar, had slept through much of the second half, as well.

She had hardly given Douglas a thought, all day, she realised. Instead she had joked and laughed with another man for much of the time and then slept on his shoulder for the rest of it.

She did feel guilty but...but...but...everyday that passed when she wasn't haunted by Douglas's memory was a tiny triumph.

When the final whistle blew, and they were shuffling out, several of the fans who had been sitting near them looked at her with amusement, and one of them said, "Enjoy the match, luv?", which got a laugh.

What had Brian thought about it all? He had seemed to enjoy the trip up and the lunch. He'd said he'd come because he had wanted to be with her, hadn't he? He had dreamt about her, he'd said.

Was he going to make a pass at her? She hoped not.

For one thing he was married, and for another when Douglas died all thought of romance had died inside her. The very thought of anyone taking his place was abhorrent to her.

She stole a glance at Brian.

He was reading the match program. He had been good company, today. He had made her laugh. Maybe the wine had made the difference, but she hoped that they could be more friendly again. She would like to see more of Marcia, too. She would ring her up tomorrow, maybe suggest a shopping trip.

'I must ring Marcia. I haven't seen her for....well, too long, anyway.'

Brian looked at her thoughtfully. Was this an olive branch?

'She would like that. She's very fond of you.'

'And I am very fond of her,' and then she surprised herself by adding, 'and I'm fond of you ,too, Brian. Do you think we can be friends, again?'

His face lit up. 'I certainly hope, so. I enjoyed today very much more than I thought I would, to be honest, even supporting your head for much of the game. Every time the crowd got to their feet in excitement, we were the only two still in our seats —'

'Oh Brian, how embarrassing! I'm sorry. Did you miss all the exciting bits?'

'Don't worry,' he laughed, 'I'll watch the highlights, later. But, yes Daphne, I am sure we can be friends. Maybe even good friends.'

And he leant across and kissed her on the cheek.

She studied him seriously. 'Brian?' she hesitated.

'Go on.'

'It's just that, well, I don't want you to think....no, it doesn't matter.'

'You don't want me to think that we can ever be more than friends. Is that what you were going to say?'

'Well, yes, something along those lines,'

Brian nodded. While Daphne had been sleeping on his shoulder at the match, her hair against his cheek, he had felt very close to her again. He had even considered telling her about his dream. He had wondered how she would react.

'Thank God I didn't,' he thought as the coach pulled into Cheltenham bus station and coughed them out into the cold damp night.

VERY TELLING

'I'm worried sick about Jim's drinking,' Viv Ward blurted out to Martine Porter, her gaze rigidly fixed on the table in front of her.

Martine's expression instantly adjusted to sympathetic concern. She knew the role she was expected to play. Had played so often before — even if never with Viv.

'Yes, I see,' Martine said softly, and then Viv did look anxiously at Martine.

'You've noticed then?'

'I'm not saying that, but...' the sentence hung unfinished between them.

'But?'

'OK.But he did fall over at our carol party.'

Viv said nothing, and Martine new better than to press her.

'I hoped everyone would think he just tripped,' Viv said at last with a sigh, staring once more at the table, 'but of course nobody did. He was swaying dangerously and slurring his speech. But if I try and stop him he gets so angry. I just don't know what to do, Martine.'

The moment she had opened the door and found Viv standing apologetically on the doorstep she guessed that this was more than a casual social visit. It was unusual for these Brits to pitch up unannounced.

'Is this a bad time, Martine?'

'Of course not, Viv. Come in. It's always good to see you.'

Now they were sitting at the scrubbed pine table of Martine's immaculate kitchen, in her pretty Listed cottage, with its garden, so beautifully maintained by her full time gardener, Percy, stretching out from the kitchen window to the gentle hills beyond.

To make room Martine had moved a pile of leaflets for the village Quilt show she was organising for September.

Graham and Martine Porter from Pittsburg, Pennsylvania had moved into Gloucestershire just three years ago, but already they were the hub around which the social life of the village revolved.

The famous British reserve had surrendered without a fight to their easy American charm.

Martine had started a Lunch club, a book group, she was a leading light in the local Amateur Dramatic Society. The Porters were lavish hosts and already had friends from one end of the County to the other.

'That's the American way, I suppose - dive in head first', the villagers said, but they were only too happy to lap up the benefits of the couple's extraordinary energy and generosity.

And such sympathetic listeners. They all agreed on that. And listeners being a magnet for talkers there was no shortage of friends and neighbours willing to share their grievances, their confidences, and their worries in this welcoming kitchen.

That's why Viv was sitting there, now, twisting her wine glass round and round in her fingers and staring at the table.

'Tell me about it, Viv', Martine said quietly. 'If you'd like to, of course.'

Viv sighed and her shoulders relaxed a little, as though some small part of the weight on them might soon begin to lift.

'I don't know where to start, Martine.'

'Well why not start when Jim started. To drink, I mean.'

'Started? I don't know — but as long as I've known him, anyway. 'An ad-man needs whisky like an engine needs oil.' That's what he used to say.'

Martine smiled 'He was on the creative side, I bet.'

'Yes. And the creatives were the worst of all. He boasted once that they had a lunch which went on till ten o'clock at night — the waiters put a screen round their table when the evening diners arrived.'

'Oh, my!'

'Friends used to say what fun he was after a few drinks. Of course, they didn't see him when he staggered home to be sick in the loo, or not going to work because of a monumental hangover.'

Viv sat staring out of the window, and Martine quietly waited.

'I've never told anyone this before.' Viv turned to Martine as if surprised she was telling it now. 'I feel such a traitor.'

'Well if you'd rather not —'

'For years we were so happy', she said wistfully, 'Jim was very generous and loving and caring. He was such a proud Dad, too. He was earning a lot of money, and we bought this lovely Georgian terrace house overlooking Blackheath — that's in South London', she explained to her American friend. 'It cost £385,000. It was a fortune, then, but we loved it.'

Now the words wouldn't stop.

'All the children were born there. Rupert was such a wonderful baby, and such a popular little boy...' Viv searched Martine's face for some kind of reaction and thought she saw the merest hint of disbelief. '...I know that's hard to believe now, Martine, but he was.' She stopped. Tears were forming in her eyes and one escaped down her cheek. She wiped it away with the back of her hand. Martine gently slid a packet of tissues towards her.

'Oh, Viv. Please don't upset yourself. We all know what a burden Rupert has been to you and Jim. And we really feel for you both. But things are getting better aren't they — with Rupert?' Is that why Viv had really come? To talk about Rupert, and not Jim's drinking?

Viv sighed heavily, took a tissue and blew her nose.

'God, I hope so!' She sniffed and blew her nose again.

Percy, who had been digging over the flower beds at the end of the garden, came down towards the open window. Whatever he was going to say to Martine he decided against it. He saw the visitor, caught Martine's almost imperceptible shake of the head, and walked past towards the back of the house, where he scrounged a cup of tea off Mrs. Holmes.

'Do you want to talk about Rupert, Viv?'

'Oh don't get me started on Rupert, Martine, you could be here for hours.'

' I've got the time if —'

'No. It's sweet of you.' Why, on earth had she mentioned Rupert, at all?

'But yes, everything crossed, it's much...calmer... at home, now. The medication seems to be working. They've put him on drugs to wean him off drugs. Ironic, isn't it?'

She sighed again. ' I wish there was a medicine that could get Jim off drink.'

She laughed bitterly. 'What a family! You must think we're a hopeless case!'

'Hey C'mon, sweetheart, that's nonsense, Viv. Graham and me ... Graham and I ... think you're real cool guys. You've got two real great kids in Sally and Jack, a lovely home, lots of friends who love you...' she tailed off. 'And if Jim does drink a bit more than's good for him, well he's had a lot to worry about, Viv. Rupert, of course...and...well, Rupert.'

'And his career, you were going to say, I daresay.' and as Martine started to protest, Viv put up her hand to stop her , 'It's alright, Martine. It's true. His career has not exactly gone to plan, either.'

'What happened Viv? You said he was doing so well.'

Martine was keenly interested in other people's careers. Particularly those that had not flourished. It was an uncharitable trait in someone usually so caring.

'Yes, he was doing very well,' Viv sighed, ' before his one bad mistake. He was the most successful copywriter at Bradshaw and Buckingham, one of the most creative advertising agencies in London. He won lots of awards. Other agencies were always trying to poach him. He had a company BMW, was made an associate director. We were very happy.'

Martine waited a few seconds before she asked, 'What was the bad mistake, Viv?'

'Another agency offered him a job with more money, and he took it.'

'And that was a mistake?' Martine sounded puzzled.

'After that nothing was the same, again. Doyle and Jennings, that was the new agency. It was a horrid place with horrid people... anyway, they hired Jim to improve the agency's creative reputation. Or that's what they said. They made him Creative Director in charge of twenty two art directors and copywriters. He'd never had such responsibility. God, he worked so hard, such terribly long hours.'

'And it didn't work out?' Martine guessed.

'Jim's just not a natural manager. He admitted that. If he didn't like the campaigns his people produced he did them himself. And much better, too.'

'I bet they hated that.' Martine said

'Yes, they did. And they hated Jim. And in the end they got him sacked.'

Viv stopped. She hadn't come to talk about Jim's crumbling career.

'Anyway,' she said emphatically, 'I'm talking far too much. Look at the time. You'll be wanting your lunch.'

'I was rather hoping you'd stop and have some with me, Viv. Just some quiche and a salad.'

Viv hesitated, 'I'd better not', then almost immediately, 'actually that would be lovely.'

'How did they get him sacked?' Martine asked when the quiche and salad were on the table.

'Long story. Fights with the creatives, who told the Chairman that Jim didn't inspire them — nasty little buggers — fights with the other directors who wanted less adventurous work. It was a relief in a way. For Jim, and for me. He got six months pay, too. I remember we went to The Savoy Grill to celebrate.'

'Good for you.'

'It was short lived, though, the celebration. His confidence had taken a battering, and constant reassurance is what creative people seem to live on. They need to be told they are special all the time.'

And Viv paused and gazed out at the garden. 'Perhaps I didn't tell him enough. Perhaps I don't tell him enough.'

'And he was still drinking a lot?' Martine steering Viv.

'Less. Despite the stress at Doyle's. I just don't think he had the time, he was working such long hours.'

Perhaps the subject triggered the thought, but Martine asked 'A little more wine, Viv?'

'No thank you. It doesn't seem...well, you know.'

'Coffee?'

'That would be nice.'

While Martine made the coffee, Viv was remembering the haunted look of her husband at that time. When he had been at Bradshaw's he had loved coming home to tell stories to the children — tucked up in bed and squeaky clean after their baths. The stories just tumbled out of his head and the kids would squeal with delight or hide under the bedclothes always pleading for 'more, more more'. Some were pretty good, Jim thought. Maybe he'd write a kids' book, one day, he'd said. But when he came home from Doyle and Jennings, the children were all asleep, and he was too tired, too dulled, too squeezed out even to talk to Viv.

She told all that to Martine, when she returned with two coffees.

'Couldn't he get his old job back?' Martine wondered. 'They must have been sorry to lose him.'

'Not sorry enough to hire him again.'

'He tried, then?'

'Yes.' Viv couldn't disguise her bitterness. 'It took a lot for Jim to swallow his pride and go cap in hand to Bradshaw's. The trouble was by then he'd been fired by Doyle and

Jennings, and he just wasn't the same man who had left three years earlier.'

Martine glanced surreptitiously at the clock on the wall. Nearly half past two, she would have to go in twenty minutes.

But she was curious to hear the rest of the story. How come the London advertising big-shot ended up here in their tiny village?

On the bottle.

'Before you go on Viv, I must just make a quick call,' she said, and immediately Viv got to her feet. 'I'm sorry, you must have so much to do —' she reached for her bag.

'No I haven't, Viv. Really. Please stay.'

'If you're sure.' Viv said.

'I'm sure.'

Then Viv sat down, and Martine disappeared to make a quiet call to cancel her hairdresser appointment.

That afternoon Viv relived for Martine the years that she hoped she had buried long ago, but the hurt and the worry of the memories were as painful as ever.

Jim had been fired from Doyle and Jennings just as the recession of 2008 was hitting the advertising business.

Viv told Martine how her heart had bled for Jim as he peddled round his portfolio, his best work now three years old, first to the top agencies, then to the next rung down and finally to any tin pot agency that would see him.

Martine could see the hurt in Viv's eyes as she recalled how his 'old friends' in the business were always at meetings when he called, or on film shoots or 'a bit busy just now' as some young secretary explained.

'Same old story,' Martine said.

'In the end a headhunter…' Viv shuddered '…God, how I hate headhunters', but she didn't amplify, 'a headhunter found an agency in Bristol which was flattered, I suppose, at the idea of hiring an ex-Bradshaw man. But Jim dug his heels in. He wasn't going to some provincial agency at half the salary and work with a bunch of second-raters. He was one of London's best copywriters. He was going to work in London. 'Once you left London,' he said, 'you'd never get back in'.

'Was he right about that?'

Viv sighed. 'Yes, probably…but we had a mortgage, the bills didn't stop coming, we had to eat.' She looked out at the garden, 'I don't think he's ever quite forgiven me for siding with that headhunter.'

'I guess you had no choice, Viv.'

'It wasn't just the job. I had to get him away from his drinking mates — a bunch of ad-men laid off during the recession who met every day in a pub near Waterloo station and drank away their redundancy money. I never knew what state he'd come home in. I would put the kids to bed as early as I could so they wouldn't see him.'

'Yep. I know all about that', Martine said, grimly.

But Viv, engulfed in her own distress, failed to register Martine's.

'Well, anyway, in the end Jim did take the job with bad grace and we sold the fine house in London for a lot of money and moved down to Bristol. We had to take Rupert out of his private school in Greenwich and put him in a Bristol Comprehensive, which I'm sure was the start of all his 'problems'.

'He started taking drugs,' Martine said. It was more a statement than a question.

'God, no! He was only nine. But he fell in with this group of boys…a sort of gang, I suppose…and he just…oh I don't know, he wasn't the same Rupert anymore. Surly, sulky, aggressive... if we asked him to do anything he'd just shrug, 'Why should I?' Viv seemed shrunken by the memory. 'The drugs came later. Anyway, Martine, I don't really want to talk about Rupert.'

'Sure. I guess the Bristol job was not a big success, for Jim?'

'No. It wasn't easy for him. A top London writer who had travelled to all those glamorous places to make TV commercials, always being flattered and wined and dined by film companies who wanted to produce his ads...it wasn't easy to adjust to a provincial agency, with pisspot local clients. That's what he called them.'

'No, it can't have been easy,' Martine agreed.

But Viv, having won Martine's sympathy, now rejected it.

'The truth is, he never tried to make a go of it. He still saw the job as a kind of holding bay, until he could land a proper job back in Town. He would take days off to go to interviews in London. He thought his colleagues in Bristol were dull and did boring work. I don't suppose he said so to their faces, but he didn't have to...they weren't stupid.' She reflected on that, 'As a matter of fact I rather liked them, and that seemed to annoy Jim, as well.'

Viv sighed. 'I'm talking too much. But I can't seem to stop.'

'That's good. A problem shared and all that.'

'I tried to share it with Jim...but he didn't want to hear. Thought I was being unsupportive.'

'And he was still drinking?'

'That didn't help.'

'I mean a lot?'

'I suppose so. No, I know so. Even though he tried to hide it from me. I think maybe that's when he started drinking secretly.'

'And he lost his job - in Bristol?'

'He had a two year contract. When it expired the agency didn't renew it.'

'By 'mutual agreement' no doubt.'

Viv had been staring down at the table as she talked, as though reading the words on the pine surface, now she glanced up at Martine. Did she detect just the hint of gloating in her tone?

'I think I've talked too much,' she said.

"I am sorry that was crass, Viv. Don't stop now, please."

Viv hesitated for a moment.

'Well, there isn't much more to say, really. Jim didn't get work in London, of course, but he found an even smaller agency in Cheltenham. That's when we moved here. But that was also short lived....the job...after 18 months or so he was replaced by a young writer who had done a copywriting course in Watford. Can you imagine how Jim felt! Replaced by a student. He was so low, he'd just given up.' she paused 'sometimes I worried that he might...' another pause '... that his health might suffer,' she finished lamely.

'Poor Jim. That's enough to make anyone drink.'

'Maybe. But I thought once he was working, free-lance, from home there wouldn't be the same opportunities to drink, or the temptations. And it wasn't long after that when Rupert's ...problem....surfaced. And that sobered us all up!'

Not for the first time, Martine marvelled at the British talent for understatement. 'Rupert's problem surfaced.' Any American Mom would have said, 'Rupert got hooked on drugs'.

'During the worst times, when Rupert was stealing and....well, the awful times...Jim was wonderful!' she said with real pride. She was pleased to be able to praise her husband, after all the tale-telling. Not just for Jim's sake, but to appease her own conscience.

'I don't know how I'd have got through those years without Jim's support. He was a real strength. He protected Sally and Jack from the worst of Rupert's excesses...he spent hour after hour with the Social Services and the Police... he'd put Rupert to bed, undress him clean him up, when he came home in such a mess. Night after night. And I think he virtually stopped drinking. I was so caught up with Rupert, too, I didn't really notice.'

'But you're worried about his drinking, now, Viv? Martine steered the conversation to the point it had begun, hours earlier.

'Yes. That's what I came to tell you about wasn't it? And instead of that I've been going on and on about the last twenty years. It's sweet of you to listen to it all. But the drinking. Yes, once Rupert was weaned off the drugs, Jim went back onto the booze. If it's not one thing it's the other.'

'Poor you!' Martine sighed.

"Oh, it's not the end of the world. I don't want anyone to feel sorry for me. Or even for Jim. On the face of it, things are much more stable, less stressful for both of us. Jim gets a certain amount of freelance commissions, mostly from Brian Woodrow, bless him - well all from Brian, actually. And he does them well, Brian tells me. Thanks to the medication Rupert seems to be winning his battles...Jack's doing brilliantly at Drama at school. His teachers say he's got a terrific talent for it. Both the acting and the directing side. Sally's doing very well at her sport —"

'Oh yes, I heard. She won some big race didn't she?' Martine jumped in.

'Yes, she did. She won the 1500 metres, for under sixteens, in the West Country championships. I don't know who she gets that from,' Viv said proudly at the thought.

Then suddenly serious again. 'Jim's drinking. I keep avoiding the topic don't I? The truth is he's ...well he's an alcoholic, and its getting worse all the time. There, I've said it.'

For once Martine was lost for the appropriate soothing words. She had a brother who had drunk himself to death in his forties. She remembered the shame, the pain, the suffering he had inflicted on their parents, his wife, his children and his little sister, Martine. She remembered the guilty sense of relief she had felt when the police came to tell them they had found his body.

'For a long time he has drunk too much in social situations.' Viv soldiered on. If she had expected a bigger reaction to her great revelation, to this weight that she carried round with her, she didn't show it. She was fully focussed on the need to get it all off her chest.

'At parties, or lunches or out with friends, he'd drink so much faster than anybody else. His glass would be empty before the host had finished filling the other people's. I suppose you've noticed that. And he'd sit there, his eyes following the bottle, willing the host to fill his glass again.

And he'd try and make a joke of it. 'I think there's a leak in this glass you gave me, Brian, ha ha', and Brian, or whoever, would refill his glass, and it would be empty again.

Then he'd start drinking before we went out. Half a tumbler of scotch —sometimes two. 'That Marcus is so bloody stingy with the drinks,' he'd say, 'need to get a head start before we go there.' I have to drive whenever we go out. Sometimes he promises to take his turn, but he's just incapable of resisting the offer of a drink. Once in a blue moon we take a taxi, but that's pretty expensive, especially if we go home after midnight. So I'm resigned now to being the chauffeur, sitting there sober while he gets drunk.'

'Then as soon as we get back home, he offers to get me a drink, 'to make up for what I missed at the party', but its just an excuse to pour himself a huge tumbler of whisky — 'to keep me company' as he puts it.'

Now Martine spoke. 'My brother was an alcoholic,' she said simply. 'I know all the tricks, all the deceptions, all the lies.'

Viv heard the bitterness in her voice, saw the pain in her eyes. Saw herself in that mirror.

'You too?'

'Yep, me too.'

They were silent for a while, but Viv couldn't resist asking, 'You said he *was* an alcoholic.' She guessed from Martine's tone that it didn't end happily.

'He died.'

'Oh, I'm so sorry Martine', she hesitated, then asked, 'from the drink?'

'Yes, from the drink,' Martine could see the anxiety in Viv's face, 'but he was a serious case, Viv. As bad as it gets, I guess. Sleeping on park benches, bottles of anything he could lay his hands on, in brown paper bags. Peeing his pants. Begging passers by for a few dollars for his next bottle. My handsome childhood hero, a wretched stinking beggar.' She stopped, the pictures in her head too painful to go on.

'That's terrible, Martine,' Viv said, reaching out to squeeze Martine's hand.

At that Martine turned to her English friend, but her mind was thousands of miles away, on a bitingly cold Pittsburgh night.

'One day he crashed headlong down some icy steps leading to a basement - where he hoped to sleep, I guess. He died of cold before anyone found him. Jim's a long way from those depths, believe me, Viv. Maybe he drinks too much, a lot of people do, but Graham was a total addict.'

'Graham?' Viv was puzzled.

'Yeah, I know. I married a man with the same name as my drunk brother. I dare say Freud would make something of that.'

They sat in silence. A dog started barking somewhere in the village, and set off another one. Yap! Yap! Yap! Woof! Woof! Woof! Yap! Yap! Yap! Woof! Woof! Woof!

When Viv had finally plucked up the courage to call on Martine that morning, she'd been desperate to share her worries with her friend. But what she really craved was some kind of reassurance. She wanted to be told that Jim's drinking wasn't as bad as she imagined. That a lot of men of his age hit the bottle quite hard, but they didn't go off the rails.

Instead she'd heard of the terrible consequences of being a slave to alcohol. And Jim was becoming a slave, she was sure. She had a son who had been a slave to a drug, she could recognize the symptoms all too well.

Jim crept away to drink furtively in his shed at the bottom of the garden, or in his office at the top of the house. She searched for bottles whenever he was out. But when she found a bottle of Famous Grouse hidden behind his desk, Jim flew into a rage. Accused her of snooping on him. 'A bloody spy! I just had a bottle there when I had that bad cold. Christ if a man couldn't take a drop of whisky when he's ill!'...and he'd stormed out of the house. It was hours before he stumbled back, crashed onto his bed fully dressed and passed out.

And now Viv had been given another awful vision.

Jim in a filthy old mac sitting on a bench in a park, with a bottle of whisky, or gin or cider whichever was cheapest... or meths...pissing in his trousers. Oh God, no.

'I must go, Martine', Viv said glumly, 'thank you for listening to all my woes, you're very kind. And thank you for the lunch, of course.'

'I'm afraid I haven't been much help, Viv.'

'No really, you have. I do feel better for letting it all out.' She got up and picked up her bag thoughtfully.

'I hope this can be our secret, Martine, I wouldn't want —'

'Don't say another word. I won't. Not to a living soul.'

'Not even to Graham?'

'Not if you don't want me to.'

Martine showed Viv to the door, and gave her a hug as they kissed goodbye.

Viv looked awkward, but thanked Martine warmly and walked away.

Was she glad she had come?

She didn't know.

Martine felt strangely exhilarated as she watched Viv walking down the village street towards her car. Why? Was it the relief of telling Viv about her brother? So often the listener it felt good to talk. More likely it was the satisfaction of realising just how lucky she was? How much better off than her friend now climbing into her old Ford Mondeo.

She had no children with drug problems. She had no children, period. That was just dandy by her. She had never seen herself as the motherly type. Perhaps Graham would like to be a father. Perhaps not. She had never asked him. Anyway he was far too busy turning the small fortune he had inherited into a significantly bigger one to be a good father.

She turned back into her chocolate-box cottage.

'Oh. Mrs Porter!'

She turned back to see Mrs. Pendleton, waddling across the road, waving some papers.

'I wonder if I could bend your ear about the Quilt Show?'

'Of course, come in. I'll put the kettle on.'

Her exhilaration subsided like one of her attempts at a bloody English sponge cake.

DRIVING A HARD BARGAIN

Ian Willard tries hard to blank the whole sorry episode from his mind, but his mind is not so obliging, and the remembering and the remorse will keep slithering to the surface.

It began the very moment Marcus Strickland pulled the torn and dirty dust sheet off the car in his stables, and immediately apologised for it.

'Well, there it is. Sorry Ian, but I did tell you it was an old wreck.'

They were standing in the disused tack room, of the fine Grade 2 listed building gazing at 'the old wreck' that had just been revealed after decades of neglect. A cloud of dust, freed from the sheet, danced in the sunlight streaming through the window. A horse whinnied in the stables.

And Marcus looked at Ian, and Ian looked at the car.

He did not speak, he did not move. An outward stillness that gave no clue to the racing of his heart and rushing in his head.

Remember those childhood drawings in which two quite different images can be discovered? It's an aeroplane in clouds, oh no, it's lion lurking in a bush.

So it was in that fusty stable that morning.

Marcus saw only a dirty, broken-down, old fashioned wreck supported on bricks, no wheels, no headlights, mildewed leather seats, a mouse nest and droppings in the footwell, the gear stick snapped off. What a mess!

And Ian saw a 3.5 litre 1938 Jaguar SS100 — a sensational find, and a small fortune in the making. What a beauty!

So why didn't he jump up and down; why didn't he cry out in joy; why didn't he embrace his companion, as all his instincts and experience would have suggested he would?

Maybe he was anxious not to raise his friend's hopes too high? Do you think?

Maybe he was anxious to keep his expectations low.

Clearly Marcus had no inkling of the value of the car standing before them. Could Ian be tempted to use that ignorance to his own advantage? No,no. He was proud of his reputation for straight dealing. But, but, but… never had the potential rewards for a little crooked dealing been so high. And never had his needs been so great.

Ian Willard did not rationalise all this in those first spellbinding seconds, but it wasn't very many minutes before an unworthy plan to take advantage of Marcus Strickland, a man he counted as a friend, was beginning to take shape.

Afterwards he tried to convince himself that in those first few minutes he had little idea of the potential profit in the car. Restoration of a classic like the Jaguar SS100 could be hugely costly, and it was plain to see how many parts were missing. But the truth was that even then he had recognised that this glorious old car — as forlorn as it looked —could be the heaven-sent answer to his ambitious but risky plans to save his business.

And, though he might not admit it even to himself, to prove he was every bit as canny as his late father.

Marcus was surprised at Ian's protracted silence. Was he trying to think of a kind way to say the car was junk?

'What do you think?' he prompted.

Ian drew in his breath, and let it out in a long thoughtful sigh.

'Well,' he walked round the car, opening and shutting the doors, peering under the chassis, feeling the upholstery. 'Well,' he repeated 'I wasn't expecting this.' He needed to probe his friend before he said any more.

'How long has it been here, Marcus? Who did it belong to? Do you know anything about the car or its history?'

'Not a lot.' Marcus said gazing at the car with distaste. 'But it has been cluttering up this tack room for donkey's years, maybe even since my father inherited the house, so presumably it was my grandfather's or, maybe one of the servant's.

Pa never drove it, I'm sure. He was a Bentley man like me. I don't know any more about it than that. Do you know what it is?'

Ian didn't look Marcus in the eye, preferring to study the door hinges.

'Yes I think I do. It was once a desirable car. It's a 1938 Jaguar, I'm pretty sure of that. The SS100. Does that mean anything to you?'

'Not a thing,' he said again, reassuring Ian, 'I had no idea Jaguar even made cars before the war.'

'Oh yes, Bill Lyons started the company in the early twenties, making side cars for motor bikes. It was called Swallow Sidecars — hence the SS. The company didn't start making their own cars until the thirties. After the war the SS was dropped for obvious reasons. A '38 SS100 would be very interesting to a collector — especially a Jaguar enthusiast.'

'You mean that it's actually worth something?' Marcus' surprise was obvious.

'Well, as it is at the moment — ' Ian let the words hang in the air.

'It's in a hell of a bad way, isn't it?' Marcus said, playing nicely into Ian's hands.

Ian studied his unworldly friend, and for a moment his resolution wavered. But only for a moment.

'Yes, it is. It's been neglected for - what? 70 years or more? But that doesn't mean it can't be restored. It does mean that restoration would be a very long and costly business, of course. The SS100 wasn't made in any quantity, so finding spare parts would be next to impossible. They would all have to be specially made by hand.'

As he was talking Ian unclipped the bonnet and folded it back over to inspect the engine. It showed some signs of rust, and most of the rubber piping and hoses had perished but was otherwise in very good condition as far as Ian could tell. He guessed the car had done very little mileage. Better and better.

'Hardly worth restoring then?' Marcus asked. 'Shall we talk about it over a glass of wine?'

'I wonder what happened to the wheels?' Ian mused, almost to himself, 'and the headlights?' He was on his knees again peering under the long rakish running board.

'Heaven only knows. They may be in one of the lofts above the garages up at the house,' Marcus casually remarked, 'There's a pile of parts. old tool boxes, that sort of thing. Wheels? I can't remember, but I haven't been up there for ages.'

Ian looked at Marcus closely, heart beating faster. Marcus was beginning to look bored, he was pulling the sheet back over the car. Ian helped him.

'Shall we go and see what you've got?' Ian said as lightly as his burning curiosity would allow. 'In those lofts?'

'By all means. But let's go and have a glass of wine, first. All this dust and grime is tickling my throat.'

'Fine.' He must bide his time, bottle up his excitement, lest it escaped to infect his friend.

As they walked the two hundred yards to Marcus' grand house, Ian's mind was racing. Would the old boy remember the name Jaguar SS100? Would he do a Google search about the car? And find out it's true value? A brief glance at his companion allayed that fear. He guessed that Marcus would have nothing to do with 'all that new fangled stuff.'

Of course, sooner or later, Marcus must learn the value of his 'old wreck.' But by then, Ian hoped to be his confidant and partner.

So when they were having their wine, he put Marcus in the picture. The picture, of course, that Ian wanted to put him in.

'Marcus, I don't want to raise your hopes too high... and I can't be sure without doing some research... is the market in classic cars holding up in this recession, for example?... are the necessary parts even possible to get?.... but a car like that one rusting in your stables, in mint condition would be very valuable.'

'You don't say? What's 'very valuable'? I mean, roughly.'

'Don't hold me to this, Marcus, but certainly over £60,000, and probably quite a bit over.'

'Good god!'

Ian laughed. 'A small fortune sitting in your garage and you didn't know. Congratulations.'

'Good heavens, well, well, well.' Then after a pause, 'In mint condition, you said, but that car's in a pretty grotty state, could it ever be in the kind of condition you're talking about? And how much would it cost to get it there?' He didn't sound very hopeful.

'That, of course, is the 64,000 dollar question.' Ian said.

'I hope not!'

Ian laughed tightly at Marcus' joke. 'Very good. But honestly I'd have to look into all that at some length. That's if you wanted me to be involved. You may know someone else who could sort the car out for you.'

It was a gamble, but he guessed a safe one.

'Of course I'd like you to be involved. I don't know anything about cars, or anybody else who does, apart from you. I mean how would it work? Would you buy the car from me, and make any profit you could? Or would I pay you to do the work and I'd get any profit?'

And that was the moment to lay his plan.

'Well that, Marcus, is the big question, isn't it? And just at the moment I've no idea. It could be that there's another solution. Let's think it through.'

'You think, I'll listen.'

'Well, normally if I find an old car, I'd buy it outright and then hope to make a profit on the restoration. But, of course, I have a pretty good idea what the restoration would cost and what I could get for the car, afterwards. But your car is in a totally different class. And in this case there are so many unknowns... you can see for yourself how much work is needed...and to interest a classic car enthusiast it would have to be absolutely authentic and immaculate, every part, every dial, every stitch... and finding or making those 70 year old parts...' he shook his head and left Marcus to finish his train of thought.

'So, It's going to cost a packet, but it's impossible to say how much.'

'That's about the size of it. I wouldn't know where to begin in offering you a fair price. Fair to me as well as you.'

'So maybe I should sell it to someone who is used to dealing with old Jaguars. Is that what you're saying?'

That was definitely not what Ian was saying!

'Not at all Marcus. Not at all. I'm saying that the profit to be made from this car, if any, is impossible to calculate right now. A real obsessive collector would happily spend a small fortune doing it up. And not so small, either. knowing there was no chance of ever seeing a return for his money.'

'Because he'd never sell it?'

'Exactly. Because he'd never sell it. But suppose for the sake of argument I offered you, say, £20,000 for the car as it is now—'

'What, in that state?' Marcus sounded incredulous.

'No, hear me out. And it cost £40,000 to restore it,' Marcus whistled through his teeth, but Ian ploughed on, 'and I sold it for say £100,000. I'd make £40,000 to your £20,000, which is not fair to you. But if it cost £50,000 to restore, and I couldn't sell it for more than £70,000, then I'd make nothing to your £20,000 which just at the moment...' again he didn't finish. He would let Marcus make his case for him.

'Which wouldn't be fair on you. Yes, I see the problem. But what's the solution, Ian. £100,000! These are unbelievable figures you're batting around. I think I need another glass of wine. How about you.'

'I won't thanks. Well I told you it was a desirable car, Marcus. But, anyway, those figures are just examples — it's all guesswork at this stage.'

He thought that by now Marcus would be ready to agree to the idea that had come into Ian's head within minutes of seeing the Jaguar.

He watched as Marcus refilled his own glass.

'Well here's a suggestion.' He stopped. He wanted to be sure he had his friend's undivided attention.

An ancient long case clock struck twelve melodious and deliberate chimes, followed soon after by a single high pitched 'ping'! from a clock on the mantelpiece.

'Yes go on old boy,' Marcus looked over his wine glass at him, 'I'm all ears.'

'In a nutshell. I restore the car and we share the profits of any sale.'

Now he had Marcus' attention.

'Go on.'

"The car would be a joint venture. Your contribution would be the car - in its present state, of course. My contribution would be the actual restoration work, which for me would be a labour of love, I admit, but a long and difficult one. It might take one year, two years or even longer."

'Then we sell the car, and split the profits?'

'Or any losses,' Ian tossed off lightly, 'but I think we're safe on that front.'

Marcus put down his glass and came across the room with his hand outstretched.

'It's a deal. Let's shake on it.'

'Whoa. Hold on, you need to sleep on it. Give it some thought.'

'No I don't. It makes perfect sense. The only thing I'm putting in is an old wreck that's been cluttering up my tack room for god knows how long. OK, it's a bit special, you say...and you're putting in a year or more's work. I think we should clinch the deal before you change your mind.'

Ian took Marcus hand with some apparent reluctance and they shook.

'There will be details to be sorted out, probably some papers to be drawn up —'

'Oh you can do all that, I'm hopeless at details. Now you will have another glass of wine, I insist, to drink to this exciting new venture.' And he went to get the bottle.

'There is one rather important detail, Marcus and the whole thing might fall through when I explain it,' he said as Marcus filled his glass.

'I hope not, I'm rather excited about this 'whole thing'.'

'I'll be honest with you, Marcus. As I said I will spend a great deal of time researching into the car, travelling to find parts, working on the restoration, but there will be costs over and above that which just at the moment Willard's can't afford.'

'Such as?'

'Well buying the parts, or having them specially crafted - which will be a costly exercise. And if my mechanics spend any time helping me to restore the car, I'll have to pay them. It all adds up.'

'I see. You want me to fund all that. Is that what you mean?'

That's precisely what Ian meant.

'Not necessarily, no. We could, perhaps, borrow the money from the bank.'

'Hmm.' Marcus clearly didn't like that idea. 'I've never borrowed a penny from a bank, and I'm not keen to start, now. I suppose that just makes me seem old fashioned to you, Ian.'

'No', just rich.' Ian thought, He took a sip from his wine glass and looked as serious as he could.

'Look, how much are we talking about, Ian? And when would you want the money?'

'I would like to give you a clear figure, but I can't. And until I've inspected the car thoroughly, done some research in the trade, I can't even give you a ball park figure. So this is what I suggest, Marcus. I take the car into my workshops and really give it the once over. See just what spare parts are needed, and the chance of finding them...and I'll talk to people I know in the classic car market. Then I will be able to come to you with some kind of figure, but in this kind of restoration there are always likely to be some unexpected expenses.'

'And what would that inspection and estimation and so on, cost? Roughly?'

'Nothing' Ian smiled. 'I would do it for my own interest, as well as to get a better idea of what I, what we I should say, are taking on. At that point you could decide to go ahead or not. It would be your choice, but either way I wouldn't charge.'

Marcus considered that.

'That sounds more than fair to me. More than fair. But I have to tell you, I want to see this through. It would be so exciting to see the old wreck—"

'You're going to have to stop calling it that.' Ian laughed.

'—to see the car under that sheet, transformed into a connoisseur's dream. And maybe make a bob or two out of it as well.'

'Many thousands, with any luck. But there's still the problem of raising the money. If you're not —'

'I'll supply the money for the restoration. Presumably, I get that back from the sale, before we split any profit?'

'Of course.' Ian hastily reassured him.

'You can't afford to. I can, and I'm not borrowing from the bank. That's final. I'm trusting you, Ian, to do us both proud.'

Surely that was the moment, the trusting moment, when Ian Willard could and should have fallen on his knees and owned up.

'Look Marcus, I haven't been straight with you. There's a bloody fortune to be made out of this Jaguar SS100 sitting in your stables. And by splitting that down the middle I'm fiddling you out of a big share that should be yours.'

He didn't say that. But he hinted.

'Look Marcus, if it turns out that there's a bigger profit in the car than I thought we may have to look at how we divide it. You more, me less.'

'No. no. A deal's a deal. Fifty-fifty, right down the middle. If it's more than we thought, great, we'll both be happy. OK?'

Ian shook his head as though he needed persuading, then he 'gave in'.

'OK.' he said simply.

He couldn't have hoped for a more satisfactory outcome. He had talked Marcus into funding the restoration, agreeing to share the profit, which Ian suspected at this early stage could be well over £100,000, and still appearing to be an 'honest Joe' in Marcus' eyes.

Unlucky Jim

Jim Ward woke with a sick headache. Jim Ward always woke with a sick headache. That is what drunks do.

But this morning the headache barely registered — swamped, as it was, by the guilt and the anguish that surged through him when the events of the previous evening came flooding back to him.

Viv at first the relaxed passenger, then the baffled one, and finally the icily furious driver. She had driven home from the film they never saw without a word, without a glance in his direction, without a speck of sympathy.

But how much could he expect, for god's sake.

Now he turned to her in the bed, to her rigid back. Was she asleep? What was that sound? A sob? Was she crying?

Oh Christ!

Jim did worry that he was sliding into alcoholism, he didn't fool himself about that, but he also believed that admitting it was the first step to recovery.

But you can't clear out the gutters unless you climb the ladder.

And Jim's first step had conspicuously not been followed by a second, third or more steps.

He had never sought professional help, he had never been to Alcoholics Anonymous, he had never talked properly to Viv about it, and most important, of course, he hadn't stopped drinking. Worse, he had started to drink secretly. And yesterday that had been his undoing.

And yet, he tried to convince himself, wasn't Viv partly to blame for yesterday's disaster? If it wasn't for that silent disapproval, he wouldn't have sneaked his whisky so furtively, and she would have driven to Cheltenham instead.

But he had slipped into his study shortly before they were due to leave, hunted out the half bottle of Laphraoig and taken a deep swig of the gorgeous golden single malt. He deserved it. He had been commendably abstemious - it was the first of the day and it was already half past six. Ah! That marvellous warm explosion in the mouth, in the throat and down into the stomach. The immediate sensation that until that moment he had not been quite complete.

Another deep swig, and then another — it would be hours before he could have another drink.

'Jim,' Viv calling up from the foot of the stairs, 'are you ready?'

'Coming!' He hollered back, took another long swig at the bottle, now two thirds empty, hid it behind his Wisden Cricketers' Almanack, and went down to the car.

Viv had walked round to the passenger seat, and he had hesitated.

'Why don't you drive?' he had suggested as casually as he could.

'No, I'm always driving,' she said before adding for good measure, 'for reasons we both know all too well.'

Such a rebuke, of course, made confession impossible. So he had settled into the driver's seat. He felt fine, better than fine. Surely the police would not be out this early looking for drunk young men at the wheel of some souped up banger, and certainly not sensible drivers like him in a Ford Mondeo. But just to be on the safe side he would take the country route and avoid the main roads.

But it was on Harp Hill, a quiet side street not a mile from the cinema, that the police car had come up behind him, flashing and wailing. He had slowed and pulled over to let it hurry past to the scene of some emergency.

But as he had slowed, so had the police car, still flashing its lights and sounding the siren. He pulled to a stop, and the blue and yellow BMW stopped behind him, its siren dying in a last mournful wail.

With thumping heart he had watched in the door mirror, as the young policeman approached.

'What's going on?' Viv had swivelled round in her seat, in surprise.

Jim lowered the window and took five great gasps of fresh air in a desperate attempt to dilute any whisky fumes on his breath as the law approached.

He was young, Jim saw, maybe 23? 25?, with a chubby pink face and a wispy blond moustache that he hoped 'made him look serious' but failed miserably to do so.

'Good evening, sir.' Polite. Giving Jim a moment's hope.

'Good evening, officer.' A little too loud, a little too taut, perhaps. 'What can I do for you?'

The constable lent a little closer, his moustache, his nose inches from Jim's face.

'Did you know, sir, that your nearside rear brake light is malfunctioning?'

'No, I didn't.' Jim looks as apologetic as he can. 'Thank you for telling me, officer.'

'It's an offence to drive a vehicle without a brake light.'

'I'll get it fixed first thing tomorrow, officer.'

Jim's hopeful repetition of 'officer' was no more persuasive than the said officer's moustache.

'Where have you come from, sir?' Not so polite, now.

'From home. Near Naunton. We, my wife and I, are going to the Cinema in Town.'

'Have you been drinking, sir?' The bombshell.

'What on earth makes you think that?' Try and bluster it out.

'I can smell alcohol on your breath.'

'You have a very sensitive nose, then officer. I had one small scotch at lunchtime - hours ago.' Damn, he should have said a glass of wine. Only a serious drinker would have scotch with his lunch. He sensed Viv sitting very still beside him.

For a moment the policeman seemed to hesitate, he leant back from the car, studying Jim, who tried to look confident and responsible, but succeeded in neither.

The moustache decided. The axe fell.

'Will you step out of the car, sir. I require you to take a breathalyser test.'

Why does bad news spread so much more quickly than good? Misfortune, it seems, has more appeal than success. Certainly, 24 hours after he had taken it, there wasn't a soul in the village who hadn't heard about 'poor old Jim's' failed breath test.

To his face, the guarded sympathy.

'That's bad luck, Jim.'

Out of his hearing, the tut-tutting.

'Suppose he'd killed someone. What then?'

Four weeks later Jim stood before three magistrates in Cheltenham with Derek Henderson at his side to support and represent him.

A costly mistake.

Not Derek's fee — he was not charging to defend his friend — but in the hefty size of the fine that the magistrates imposed on Jim, almost certainly because of Derek's misguided intervention.

Derek is an able and confident solicitor, but his strengths – property rights, divorce law and family disputes – were singly unsuited to the occasion.

He was familiar with the court, of course, but was disappointed to find that he knew neither of the two women nor the man sitting on the bench that morning, all who sat almost exclusively on traffic offences.

He was also quite unprepared for the speed with which the cases were heard and decided. There was none of the careful consideration and detailed argument that he was used to in family disputes. There were no representatives from the social services, none from the local authority and precious little legal representation, either.

Some of the those before the bench —nearly all for drink driving offences — spoke for themselves, and others called on a duty solicitor provided by the court to speak for them.

Only Jim had his own lawyer.

Most cases were heard in under 10 minutes. A police officer would read an account of the arrest, and the result of the blood test, the senior magistrate would ask if the defendant had anything to say, whereupon he (they were nearly all men) would mumble their excuses or apologies, and the magistrates would whisper together for a few seconds, and announce their verdict.

'The defendant will be banned from driving any motor vehicle on the public highway for xx months and must pay a fine of £xxx before leaving the court this morning. You may stand down. Next case please.'

The xx ban was usually 12 months.

The £xxx fine was typically about £200 - £300.

Jim's case took nearly 25 minutes, which had the magistrates glancing impatiently at their watches long before the end.

Derek's determination to do the very best for his friend was well intentioned — but, to be kind, counterproductive.

Not only did he speak on Jim's behalf for far too long and too theatrically, but as he spoke Jim could feel the magistrates mentally upgrading the fine they would eventually impose on him.

First of all, the defendant could afford to engage his own lawyer, and by the look of him an expensive one, and secondly in his attempt to paint a picture of Jim's untainted and worthy character, Derek succeeded only in impressing on the minds of the Bench, Jim's successful and privileged lifestyle in a wealthy and exclusive community.

And a boozer, to boot.

In order to illustrate how unusual it was for Jim to have driven a car when he had been drinking, Derek expanded at some length on how often he had *not* done so.

His client, he explained, was in a profession, advertising, (Jim could sense the bench's disapproval) that had a culture of heavy drinking (more disapproval) and yet never before had his client even thought of getting behind the wheel of a motorcar under the influence of drink, no matter how often that had occurred. And on this occasion he had only done so because he had been quite unaware that he was anywhere near the legal limit, or, of course he would not have driven that afternoon, and would not be standing deeply remorseful before their Worships this morning'.

'He very much regrets his action,' Derek finally concluded, 'and apologises sincerely to the court. In these circumstances I hope your worships will agree that the usual sentence in these cases would be inappropriate.' He sat down.

Whisper, whisper on the bench, a full two minutes longer than usual. Was that a good sign, Ian wondered hopefully.

Then the verdict.

'Mr. Ward,' the senior magistrate intoned, glancing sternly over his spectacles, 'your counsel has suggested that the usual sentence in these cases would not be appropriate in yours. He is correct.'

Jim's elation survived for a full two seconds.

'You were driving a vehicle with almost twice the legal limit of alcohol in your blood. This demonstrates a substantial alcoholic intake, as you must have been fully aware — despite your counsel's somewhat discursive plea,' glancing irritably at Derek. 'You are not an irresponsible young man, who might be egged on to drink too much by his friends. Your actions cannot be excused in any degree. You will be banned from driving a motor vehicle on the public highway for a period of eighteen months and you must pay a fine of one thousand five hundred pounds before you leave the court this morning. If you cannot pay that sum today, you will be given a schedule by which time payments must be made. You may stand down. Next case please.'

'£1,500! Five times as much as anyone else this morning. And the longest ban. Jesus, Derek!'

They were sitting in a pub not a hundred yards from the Magistrate's Court, Derek nursing an orange juice and Jim a triple scotch — God he needed it!

Derek was subdued. He knew he had miscalculated the occasion, knew he had done his friend no favours, but he certainly wasn't going to admit as much.

'It could have been worse, Jim.' And as Jim started to protest, held up his hand. 'No, really it could. To be honest I thought you would be given a two-year ban. You were nearly twice the limit, remember — that usually makes all the difference.'

'I didn't realise you were such an expert in traffic offences.' Jim said bitterly. Then he relented a little. 'Anyway, thanks for your efforts, Derek.'

'Yeah. It s'OK. A-OK Ward, man.' Derek reverted to the school slang they'd learned all those years ago, in a doomed attempt to lighten the mood, to re-establish the bond.

Jim just sighed and said, 'But hell, you made me sound bloody wealthy. £1,500!'

'I may have overdone that a tad, I admit that — but I didn't want you to come across as some kind of irresponsible bum alcoholic. Anyway, look at you; expensive suit, white shirt, silk tie. When did you ever wear a tie? Of course you look prosperous.'

'And what was all that guff about advertising and all the booze sloshing about in it? OK, you said I had never drunk and driven before — not true by the way — despite numerous temptations. Implication; I'm a drunk. But a considerate drunk.'

Derek shifted uncomfortably in his chair.

'Well, I think their worships took my point on board.' He looked at his watch. 'I must be getting back to the office.' He started to rise, but sat down again when Jim spoke more seriously. 'Derek, to be honest that £1,500 is a killer. Look, I've know you for, what 35? 40 years? I can tell you things I wouldn't tell anybody else.'

Derek braced himself for a confidence.

'And I hope you'll keep anything I say between ourselves.' But before Derek could answer, Jim ploughed on.

'Money is tight in that wealthy middle class household you painted so vividly for their snotty 'worships'. Bloody tight. To be honest I'm just not getting enough work coming in as it is, and now I can't drive it will be harder than ever to find it. The kids constantly need funds for school projects, new clothes...' and for the next five minutes Jim told Derek why he couldn't possibly pay the £1,500 fine. The cheque that he had written for £500 in the court not an hour before would not be honoured.

'Are you saying the cheque will bounce?' Derek was horrified, he had agreed to act as surety for his friend finding the remaining £1,000. 'Jim, for God's sake, you can't default on a court fine, you'll get into all kinds of hot water. Me, too. This is serious, Jim.'

'I know that - but what can I do. I haven't got the money.'

'We could have asked for more time to pay, and smaller amounts —'

'I just wanted to get out of that damn building as soon as I could. And I want to pay the fine off as soon as I can.'

'But you can't.'

'Derek, could you lend me the money. The £1,500?' No beating about the bush.

Derek studied his friend, dispassionately. If Jim defaulted on his payment, the court would chase him, as guarantor, for the money and Jim knew it. He had given three hours of his expensive time, free, to help Jim and this was all the thanks he got.

'Look, Derek, just one good commission and I can repay the lot. It's just a short term loan, I can promise you that.'

Jim's sudden optimism didn't sit easily with his earlier pleas of poverty, but Derek was beginning to suspect that Jim Ward was losing touch with reality beneath a fog of whisky fumes.

'I must go.' He said rising.

'And the money?'

'I'll think about it.'

'There's not much time, Derek. That cheque could be presented today—'

'I'll send you the £500, today. I'll think long and hard about the other £1,000.'

'Good man. You won't regret it.' Jim called to the closing door. Then he went and ordered another double malt.

'Yeah. it s'OK. A-OK , Henderson, man,' he said to no one in particular.

Just another drunk, the barman thought.

The Gloucester Daily Times would not normally have commented on a drink driving ban — unless the case involved a death or serious injury. And it was just by chance that Jack Denton, their crime reporter — so called, though he doubled as a sports reporter, and a local affairs reporter — having nothing better to do, wandered into the magistrates court and witnessed Derek Henderson's clumsy intervention on behalf of Jim Ward.

Back at the office he told the story as a joke. Of course he exaggerated the solicitor's incompetence, and revelled in every burst of laughter it provoked.

Then Penelope Draper asked who this incompetent solicitor was, and Jack Denton who had jotted down the names out of habit, glanced at his notes.

'Henderson. But if you're looking for a solicitor to defend your pornography charge, Penny, I'd think again.'

'Very funny, but when I nail you for sexual harassment, he might be just the man you need.'

It was a few minutes later that Penelope Draper wondered if it could be the same Henderson, who had written the letter they had published in the paper. Common enough name, and the letter had given no indication that he was a solicitor.

She had had no luck in pinning him down for an interview after he had returned from his holiday. He had adamantly refused to meet her or even talk on the telephone. Pity, it might have made a witty piece.

It was a long shot, but she idly Googled solicitors in Gloucester and found Macklin, Winter and Henderson. Could it be the same one?

She dialled the number.

'Macklin Winter and Henderson. Good morning.'

'Oh good morning. I was wondering if I'd got the right Henderson. Is it Mr. Derek Henderson?'

'Yes, it is. Shall I see if he is in?'

'Mr Henderson, I believe, lives near Naunton, and has recently visited The Galapagos islands? I am just checking that this is the same Mr. Henderson that I spoke to before.'

'Excuse me, who is this speaking?'

'My name is Penelope Draper, from The Gloucester Daily Times. I believe we published one of his letters in our paper, and I was anxious to follow up our report.'

'I am sorry, Mr Henderson is not available to comment.'

The receptionist had strict instructions about that. No one in the office was unaware of the tensions the letter had caused in the firm, and that the sooner it was forgotten the better. But to Penelope Draper the response merely confirmed her suspicions.

'It sounds as though you have been ordered to say that. Are you protecting Mr Henderson? What from?'

'I have nothing more to say. Goodbye.'

'If our article embarrassed Mr. Henderson, perhaps we could redress the balance.'

But she had been cut off.

'Or on the other hand,' Miss Draper mused, 'perhaps we could embarrass him a little more.'

At lunch in the canteen she casually asked Jack Denton if he was going to write up the story about the solicitor who talked up his client's fine.

'God no. It was just a bit of a laugh.'

'Mind if I do, you made it sound very funny, Jack.' She gave him her winning smile — or what she had decided was her winning smile in front of her bathroom mirror.

He studied her suspiciously. What was she up to? 'If you can get that past Bert you're a better man than I am.' Albert Wishart, editor of the paper would give it short thrift, he was sure of that.

'Yes I am,' she said, and added to his puzzled face, 'a better man than you are.'

'Do you want to come into the Gents to prove that, my dear?' he ogled.

She left him shovelling down great spoonfuls of sticky toffee pudding, and went back to her computer.

She knew Denton's days at the paper were numbered. Albert Wishart had implied, in his endlessly convoluted way, that she could take over some of his assignments. But no thank you, she had her eyes on London. Everything she wrote for The Gloucester Daily Times was done to impress some distant editor in Fleet Street.

She searched out Derek Henderson's home number, taken from the letter published in the paper, and dialled.

The telephone rang for some time, and Penelope was about to hang up when a young girl answered. 'Hello?'

'Hello, who is that?'

'My name's Jade Henderson. Do you want to talk to mummy, because she's not here at the moment?'

'My name is Penny, I have spoken to your father. He's a solicitor isn't he, Jade?'

'Yes, but he's at work.'

'And where does he work, do you remember?'

'In Gloucester. In Westgate Street.'

'That's right. How clever of you. How old are you Jade?"

'I'm nine and a half.'

'And did mummy and daddy have a lovely holiday in the Galapagos Islands?'

Would this young girl remember a name like that?

'Peter and I went, too. It wasn't just mummy and daddy.' She sounded surprised that Penny didn't know this.

'How lucky you are. Do you know anyone called James Ward, Jade?'

'No. I've got an uncle Jim Ward, though he's not really my uncle, he's a friend of daddy and mummy.'

That was all she needed. She rang off.

Then she turned to her computer. Whose style would she imitate today? What award winning writer would hammer out the droll prose, the cutting wit that would appear under her name in tomorrow's paper? Could this be the piece that caught the eye of a national editor? That won a prize for original writing at the local newspaper awards?

But by the time Albert Wishart's blue pencil had finished with the masterpiece, he had reduced it to a single paragraph and Penelope Draper nearly to tears.

'This is a Gloucester paper for Gloucester people. They want to know about local weather, the local football teams, weddings, road works, where they'll find the best bargains.... if they want arty-farty reports like this,' he jabbed his pencil at Penny's article, 'they can buy The Daily Mail, The Guardian or whatever. No doubt you think you're too clever for this paper —'

'No I don't Albert. Not at all. I know how much you've taught me.'

'— but as long as you're here you do things my way.' He softened a little, she was a bloody attractive girl, after all. 'You'll learn. You are coming along OK. In a few years you might even be after *my* job.' He laughed as though the idea was unthinkable.

It certainly was to her.

The article she resubmitted to Albert was, to her mind, a great opportunity missed,

but he liked it.

'Better.' He said.

It appeared as a small paragraph in the Diary page. There was not even a subhead.

Readers may remember a local solicitor, a Mr Derek Henderson from N***** who asked his friends and colleagues to appraise, him warts and all. It provoked a lively correspondence in this paper. Well today Mr Henderson defended a friend, a Mr. James Ward, on a drinks-driving charge at Gloucester Magistrates Court. Mr Ward received an 18 month driving ban and a fine of**

£1,500. By far the stiffest penalty of the day.

One wonders what Mr. Ward would say about his 'friend', now!

The paragraph was 'brought to the attention' of Bruce Macklin, Senior Partner, who tut-tutted and sighed and shook his head when he showed it to Derek.

Derek was apoplectic. His professional integrity and ability were impugned and he wrote furiously to the Editor of the Gloucester Daily Times, insisting on a printed apology and hinting at legal action.

Two days later Albert Wishart was put through to his office.

'Mr Henderson, I'm Albert Wishart, editor of the Gloucester —'

'I know who you are.'

'Yes, well I've got your letter in front of me. Writing provocative letters seems to be your thing. My advice would be to write less of them.'

'I'm not interested in your advice, I want an apology printed in the paper.'

'What for? We published your first letter in good faith at the request of its owner, and as for the drink driving business the less said about that the better for you, I'd say.'

'Are you going to print an apology?'

'No. My legal department says you haven't a leg to stand on. Good day.'

'Just a minute, Wishart. What does your 'legal department' say about a reporter harassing a nine year old girl.'

'What are you talking about?'

'I am talking about a woman called Penny, who rang our house and bullied my young daughter. What's your name? How old are you? What does Daddy do? Is he a solicitor? Where does Daddy work? Had I been to the Galapagos, recently, did I know James Ward, Did she know about Daddy's letter in the paper? The poor girl was very upset. Is that acceptable practice for your paper?'

There was a silence.

'Nothing to say, Mr Wishart?'

'Plenty. But not to you. I will reserve that for our reporter. I apologise for her behaviour. Good afternoon.' He rang off.

Jim Ward was drinking straight from a bottle of cheap whisky, when Rupert walked into his 'office', at ten in the morning. It was impossible to tell which of the two was the more shocked and embarrassed; the father or the son.

Jim scrambled to hide the bottle, splashing some whisky on his shirt. But then replaced the bottle rather unsteadily back on the desk.

'Sorry Dad,' the boy mumbled, 'I didn't know...' But then he didn't know what he didn't know, and dried up. He started to leave the room.

'Did you want something, Rupert?'

Rupert offered the newspaper he had in his hand. 'I saw this piece about you in the local paper, that's all.'

His father took the paper, read the paragraph about his drink driving ban, and handed it back.

'He won't like that.' He laughed with some bitterness, and also some satisfaction.

Derek Henderson had done neither of them any favours in court.

'I just thought you would like to see it.' Again he started for the door.

'Rupert?'

The son turned to the father. What now?

Jim indicated the bottle, briefly.

'Just elevenses.'

Rupert nodded awkwardly.

'No need to tell your mother.'

'No, dad.'

'She'll only nag.' Conspirators, father and son. Sharing secrets.

Rupert hesitated at the door, maybe his father's tone encouraged him.

'Dad?'

Jim looked at Rupert - the desperately thin, awkward boy who had nearly died from drugs, and felt a surge of love for him.

'What is it Rupert?'

'It's just... ,' but his courage faltered, 'it's nothing, really.'

Jim sighed, walked round the desk, holding it, Rupert noticed, for support, and closed the door.

'Come and sit down, tell me what's on your mind.' Just a hint of defensive aggression that alerted Rupert.

'You'll only get angry, dad.'

'Try me.'

But Rupert stared mutely at the carpet.

'You are not back on the drugs, again, are you?'

Stung by the blind injustice of these words, Rupert turned on his father with all the righteous indignation of a wronged 17 year-old.

'NO! I am NOT back on drugs. This is not about me. It's about you. It's you that you should be worried about, not me!'

'Go on, then, spit it out.'

'You know what I mean.'

'Not precisely, no.'

Rupert hesitated. Could his father really be blind to the extent of his drinking problem. Just elevenses, for God's sake. But then hadn't his own mind refused to admit he had a drug problem?

'I was just thinking, Dad, about the drug thing, since you mentioned it. That was bad stuff, very bad stuff,' he shuddered at the memory, 'for everybody — you, mum, Jack and Sally — as much as me. I know that.' He gazed at his feet. 'I wouldn't have got through it, if you hadn't all helped me; that and the medication — but you specially, dad. I haven't forgotten all the time you spent mopping me up...and... and ... well, everything, else.'

'It was a bad time, Rupert, but fingers crossed.'

'Anyway, thank you, Dad. I never said that.'

Jim could feel tears coming to his eyes, they did that so easily nowadays.

'It's what dad's are for, Rupert.'

They were silent, each with memories, best forgotten.

'Is that what you wanted to say?'

Rupert hesitated. It would be so easy to walk away, but if he didn't say something now, would he ever?

'Well, not really.'

'You think I drink, too much? Is that it?'

Rupert tried to gauge his father's tone. Was he angry? Would he deny it, or even admit it.

'I suppose I do, in a way, yes,' he said warily.

'What way?'

'Well, like this drink driving thing, and coming home, you know, sort of drunk, and like all the wine bottles we recycle every week, and... well...,' he motioned at the whisky bottle, 'elevenses.'

Jim gazed at his earnest son. He felt dog tired, he felt like a drink, he could see the bottle, sense the bottle, beckoning him.

'You're right, Rupert, I do drink too much. I admit it. Hands up,' and he reached out for the bottle and took a swig, 'there, happy?'

Rupert scuffed at the carpet with his foot.

'It's an addiction, I guess,' he mumbled, 'the drinking, like my drugs.'

'Oh no, Rupert. Not like your drugs. Not like your drugs one little bit.' He remembered the scheming, stealing, vomiting, lying, near-starving Rupert, totally in the power of the little white powders. How could his son compare —

'No, Dad. I didn't mean...well, you know...it's just that I thought that…well, that maybe someone, something, could help you… like,well, you helped me.' He was determined to get this off his chest, he would plough on.

'I think you'll find that they haven't invented pills to stop you drinking.'

Not like the pills that controlled his son's drug addiction, he meant.

'I mean like, you know, Alcoholics Anonymous or something.'

'I said I drink too much, Rupert,' he snapped, 'I didn't say I was an alcoholic.'

'No Dad.'

Jim could see the disbelief in his son's eyes, and feel the tears welling up, again, in his own eyes. Why did he cry so easily? And then the tears were spilling over and pouring down his cheeks. He sat at his desk in front of his son and sobbed.

Rupert was frozen in his chair. Pinned to his seat by embarrassment, love and alarm.

After a while Jim's sobs morphed into one long drawn out sigh, he wiped his eyes, blew his nose loudly into a tissue and released his son from his paralysis.

'Thanks for showing me the paper, Rupert.'

And Rupert left the room.

Anyone for menace

From the baseline Michael Hurst lobs the ball over Brian Woodrow's head.

Ah, but for once his much lauded accuracy has deserted him.

He has miscalculated the trajectory by a whisker, and how could he possibly calculate the consequences?

Brian tottering backwards leaps and smashes wildly at the ball arcing above him, and rather to his surprise hits it — THWANCK! — right off the meat of the racket. The ball hurtles back across the net.

Freeze frame! Stop right there - a split second before the incident which must surely inflame the carefully masked hostility between two of the players on the tennis court that afternoon.

Now with the ball frozen in mid air, the four players stuck in gravity-defying poses, we have all of time to describe the tableau, the setting, the characters in it and their relationships.

On the right of the net, Brian and Marcia Woodrow who you know.

On the left of the net, Michael and Marjorie Hurst, who you don't.

The tennis court is theirs. Behind the court, behind the sweeping lawn, sprinkled now with immobilised friends in white, we can see part of their large, draughty Victorian villa.

The Hursts have six extrovert children who, in turn, have four dogs, several cats, two ponies in the paddock, rabbits in cages, two escaped hamsters skittering around under the floorboards and almost as many friends as their 'ma and pops'.

The large house is seldom large enough.

Michael and Marjorie Hurst make a very strong case for the attraction of opposites.

Michael first.

Oozing with vitality, Michael is a man who finds stopping for a second difficult. We've stopped him in our tableau, of course, but look how, even now, he seems coiled for action. Look how the racket is stretched out to the limit in front of him, how his left leg is thrust out behind him, his lively eyes fixed on the ball frozen over the net.

Michael Hurst is NOT an antiques dealer. And nothing riles him more than being called one. He protests, perhaps a little too often, that he does NOT 'deal' in antiques, like some horse trader. No, he rescues neglected, mostly Georgian, furniture, smothers it with love — and the very finest polish —-restores it (a tricky area — best avoided) to its erstwhile elegance, and there it stands, in one of his three discreet showrooms, until someone, captivated by his irresistible enthusiasm, and who can afford to pay his breathtaking prices, is allowed to take it away.

Now, does that sound like an antiques dealer? Well if it does you'd best not say so in front of Michael Hurst.

Michael has appeared several times on The Antiques Roadshow where his infectious enthusiasm and easy manner have made him one of the show's more popular contributors, and certainly done nothing to harm the hefty price tags hanging in his showrooms.

But he is so much more than a lover of antiques. Michael is brimming with enthusiasms.

He is passionate about old cars, ballet, theatre, hiking, cycling, skiing and flying his micro-light; he loves gardening and plants and butterflies - an active member in the local branch of Butterfly Conservation, any Sunday morning might find him and fellow lepidopterists clearing or planting to conserve or encourage some ever diminishing species.

He cooks. He reads. He talks. How he talks - only too happy to share his thoughts on anything from comparative religions to honey fungus.

Despite all this, he is popular.

His friends fall over themselves to invite him (and Marjorie, of course) to their parties, picnics, dinners, children's weddings, to the races at Cheltenham, to Glyndebourne, to their 'places' in The Dordogne or Tuscany or the Caribbean. They regretfully decline more invitations due to prior engagements than most people receive invitations.

But perhaps Michael Hurst's greatest love, after his young family and his old furniture, is tennis. The court at Walnut House — named not after any trees in the garden, but Michael's favourite veneer — is in constant use. The children play for hours on end, the wives play every Tuesday and Thursday, there's a serious men's doubles at least twice a week, and then there are the tennis parties, like the one still frozen, when a dozen or more friends may turn up with their rackets, and loll on the lawn, the kids sipping lemonade, the grown-ups getting tipsy on Pimms waiting for their turn to muff their shots and giggle on the court.

Michael is comfortably the best player. He represented Bristol University, (his failure to persuade any of three Oxford colleges to accept him still rankles) and even now plays occasionally for the county seniors - now, alas, in the second or third team.

He has a vicious spinning serve which he employs only sparingly at home, in deference to his friends' almost total inability to return it.

In the men's doubles matches he partners the weakest player — Charles Chandler — and sometimes contrives to let their opponents win without them suspecting.

Not to mince matters, Michael Hurst is a good egg. His fizzing energy sparks life into all but the most morose. He is a social jump lead.

Compare and contrast - Marjorie.

Marjorie Hurst is the only player in our frozen tableau who is unlikely to collapse onto the court when gravity is restored - standing at the net, her two size ten feet planted firmly under her, the racket across her heavy torso like a Zulu shield.

She is a very large woman. Shorter than Michael by just an inch, and wider by several.

She insists that she is NOT six feet tall with the same intensity that her husband insists that he is NOT an antiques dealer, and she takes umbrage should anyone presume that she is, which might suggest that she is uncomfortable with her height, but for the fact that she looks down her nose at all short people, and especially short men.

Marjorie's nose is a prominent feature on a broad face, and looking down it a defining characteristic. Very few can survive her critical inspection unscathed, except Michael and her darling children, who, perhaps luckily for them, share more of their father's good nature.

Her own father, a Bishop who, Marjorie claims, narrowly missed the Archbishopric of York, instilled in his daughter not so much a love of God as a disdain for man and his the many shortcomings. And no one is quicker to recognize their faults.

Charitable friends describe her as very serious, others would find sanctimonious and humourless more appropriate.

She has a clearly defined hierarchy of those worthy of her attentions - and to some it is tediously predictable.

She most approves of those in the Church, the Law and Medicine.... then the Army and Royal Navy (but definitely not the RAF - Royal though it may be).

The Civil Service she considers an acceptable career, but industry, business and The City are only tolerable as a necessary evil.

Quite where an antique dealer, who isn't — even one as respected as Michael — fits into her approval ranking is hard to guess, but Marjorie is quite capable of accommodating contrary positions if it suits her.

She appears to share her husband's love of classical music, theatre and literature, if sufficiently serious.

But she reserves the deepest distaste for anybody in the less exalted creative fields. The 'so-called' creative fields, as she calls them.

So don't put your daughter on the stage, don't make a living in journalism, marketing and especially not advertising, avoid anything to do with modern dance, modern theatre, popular music, most television, and don't even mention modern art if you want to keep in the good books of Marjorie Hurst.

And few people want to offend her if only because they enjoy her husband's company so much.

So abundant are the invitations that fall onto the doormat of Walnut House, it would be surprising if she did not consider herself well liked. But, as Brian Woodrow often spitefully wonders, how quickly would they dry up if anything happened to Michael — anything like death, for instance.

But Michael is still very much alive and seems devoted to his unsmiling wife. He doesn't take offence when she rebukes him for the occasional extravagance. Like the time he brought home a bottle of Bollinger Grand Annee 1999 to celebrate the sale of a 'magnificent and rare' Queen Anne bureau-bookcase for £32,000. The bottle cost £78, modest alongside the £13,400 profit on the bookcase, but Marjorie was horrified. She couldn't possibly enjoy a champagne, she insisted, that cost three times as much as a perfectly acceptable one. So Michael had driven back to the smart off-licence in Winchcombe and swapped the Bollinger for a 2003 vintage Moet and Chandon which cost £49 in the shop, but had miraculously reduced to £24.50 by the time he arrived home.

As matriarch of the family household it is Marjorie's duty to husband its finances, and she does it with scrupulous care. The fact that Michael's business is accumulating money faster than they could spend it, unless he develops a sudden passion for a fleet of Ferraris or a 100-foot luxury yacht, which with Michael is never entirely off the cards, is beside the point.

Indulgence is a weakness. Unnecessary indulgence is sinful. Her father drummed that into the young Marjorie long ago.

But like many of the wealthy but thrifty there is no consistency in Marjorie Hurst's endless 'looking after the pennies'.

She will haggle over the price of a cabbage, but reserve seats at the Opera that would buy half a field of cabbages. They will travel business class half way round the world and then, ragged and tired after a flight from Singapore, stand for 30 minutes at a bus stop at Bristol Airport at six in the morning in the pouring rain and laden down with luggage while their fellow passengers fall with relief into taxis.

Is this an uncharitable picture of Marjorie Hurst? It must be.

After all, she is a caring and effective mother, if the children are any measure. All are boisterous, but kindly, fair and polite. The atmosphere in Walnut house is certainly hectic but undeniably happy. Michael Hurst can't take all the credit for that.

But at least one of the players frozen in our picture, flailing backwards surely about to land awkwardly on his backside, would not argue with the description of Marjorie Hurst. Brian Woodrow could have written it himself.

Marjorie and Brian certainly do not make a case for the attraction of opposites. Each finds the other thoroughly unlikeable.(In which respect, of course, they are not so much opposite as similar.)

His wife and today his playing partner, Marcia, is far less critical of Marjorie, which will come as no surprise to those who have met Brian and Marcia already. But even magnanimous Marcia finds Marjorie chilly and distant, seldom if ever instigating a conversation, though perfectly polite when Marcia speaks to her first.

Nothing generates dislike more than the perception of being disliked. Brian believes that Marjorie is hostile to him, and is inclined to return the animosity, which Marjorie senses and returns, and so the spiral grows.

Marjorie thinks that Brian is below the salt,.

In the first place he is in one of those 'so-called' creative industries. She is not sure what he does, but it is a trivial occupation, she knows that much. And she feels that he is a trivial person, always ready with a 'quip', as she calls them, always 'making light' never properly serious. She regrets that Michael and Brian have several interests and activities in common.

Brian feels this unspoken censure — probably exaggerates it but certainly resents it.

Hasn't he built up a successful and respected advertising and graphics design company in Cheltenham? Yes, he has. And doesn't this Company own a very substantial late Georgian detached house in the city centre where he employs 36 staff - working for both local and national clients? Yes, it does.

And no, it has not been accomplished without setbacks and struggle.

He and a friend, Jimmy Wilson started the company in the one bedroom flat they had shared while at their art college, called it Woodrow Wilson (which they thought droll) and struggled to make a living with scant success.

After two discouraging years Wilson left to join a large agency in Bristol, and Brian, now called Woodrow Design, soldiered on alone, working late into the night and often for little fee, to build up a portfolio that would attract the bigger fishes.

His bank statements were conspicuously red when he made the breakthrough.

It had come one night when he fell asleep slumped over his drawing board and was woken by a dustcart collecting bottles at dawn.

He threw some cold water on his tired eyes, and went back to the drawing board, literally and metaphorically. He ripped off the design he had gone to sleep over, and started again on the mailing shot that was to catch the eye of his first major client.

Over the years the naive college designer had become the persuasive executive, the tough businessman, and the inspiration for a team of talented but often temperamental designers, writers and art directors.

And Woodrow Design now offered its enviable list of clients a full design, marketing and advertising service.

Not a trivial achievement, he reckoned, whatever the holier-than-thou Marjorie Hurst might think.

Despite their dislike, these two antagonists had to observe a veneer of politeness towards each other, as they were not infrequently in each other's company. The Hursts invited the Woodrows, the Woodrows invited the Hursts. To parties, to suppers and, like the one still frozen, to tennis matches.

Michael and Brian are both members of a Cheltenham Business Forum, which meets once a month to discuss local trading opportunities and to encourage young entrepreneurs. Both men enjoy these meetings, and especially the lunch that follows in the private room of an excellent local restaurant. Both are members of an

Investment club, which also meets in the private room of a pub, and also entails a lunch of considerable length.

Such are the petty jealousies and misunderstandings that can flourish in a small, close community and which do no credit to either person. Each diminishes himself in endlessly diminishing the other.

But back to the frozen tennis match - and ACTION!

Unfreeze Michael as he races across court, unfreeze Brian as he topples back after his smash, but doesn't fall, unfreeze Marcia as she follows the flying ball, and unfreeze Marjorie as she stands frozen as the ball smashes into her face.

Her sunglasses explode and cut deep into her eyebrow and cheek, her racket drops to the floor, and Marjorie follows it, like a felled oak, slumping onto her broad knees, hands over her face as if to ward off further blows.

Stricken with remorse Brian has leaped the net and is at her side even before Michael.

'Oh God, Marjorie. I'm so sorry.' He sees blood pouring down her cheek, but her hands are hiding the wound. He doesn't know what to do. He can't think what to say. Except 'I'm so sorry.'

'Let me have a look, darling.' Michael is supporting his wife with one arm and gently moving her hands from her face with the other. Blood is streaming from two deep cuts, one above the eye and one just below. The cut in her cheek is deep, but the cut just above the eye less so. The eye itself appears unharmed. Thank God thinks Brian as he hovers over Marjorie.

She will think he hit the ball at her on purpose. Did he? he wonders.

No, no. It was as much as he could do to hit the ball at all, let alone guide it.

Marjorie is carefully supported to a garden seat on the lawn, surrounded by fuss and friends. Her face is bruising already and her nose is swollen. Barry Dennis takes over. He is a doctor.

He removes the towel that Marjorie has been holding to the cuts.

'Hmm, That will have to be stitched up, today, Marjorie. Michael you need to get her to A & E at the General in Cheltenham, or closer, The Moore Cottage Hospital in Bourton. I'll call to see if there's anybody who can do it on a Saturday afternoon.' He gently feels her red swollen nose 'Does that hurt?'

'A bit' she says.

'I think it is just bruised, not broken, we'll know better when the swelling goes down. But you will have two lovely black eyes, I'm afraid.'

'Two?' says Marjorie with a hint of pride.

' 'Fraid so.'

The crowd, hovering round this consultation like a class of medical students, nod in agreement.

'I'm so sorry.' Brian repeats 'I'm surprised I even hit the ball. I wish I hadn't, now.' he appeals to the crowd, hoping for absolution.

It comes from the last place he expects it.

'It wasn't your fault Brian, it was an accident.' Marjorie tells him.

'Yes, but I still feel awful about it.'

'Well don't.'

Everyone is moving to the house, Michael supporting Marjorie, Barry Dennis talking to the Cottage Hospital on his mobile phone. Yes, they can do the stitching as soon as the patient gets there.

'I'll go with you' Brian finds himself saying in a concerned voice, but is relieved when the offer is declined.

'Nothing you can do - but thanks for the thought.' Michael says.

And soon he is driving his wife to Bourton.

Brian Woodrow watches them drive away and wonders if he might have misjudged Marjorie Hurst.

Just a little.

Driven to despair

'The moment I set eyes on that bloody car'...

Ian Willard had no need to complete the sentence. His heavy sigh, the shaking of the head, his forlorn expression was eloquent enough.

And his friends had heard his lament too often, knew the story too well.

Yes, It had gripped the village for several weeks but now they knew the ending, now the camera crews had left. Now they had heard enough.

But if he was honest with himself — or, more to the point had been honest with Marcus Strickland — Ian's tale of woe should have been a tale of triumph.

Once upon a time it might have been a fairy story.

The truth is that the moment Ian set eyes on that bloody car, that bloody wonderful car in Marcus Strickland's stables, he had been in a state of such excitement he could barely sleep.

Every day he found some excuse to return and admire the prize, often when he knew Marcus and Julia would not be there. No point in rousing suspicions.

And what a fuss he made transporting the car to his

workshops. 'Careful! Careful! Watch that! Mind this! Careful there!'

And how he had glowed with pleasure and pride once the precious 1938 Jaguar was crouching behind a makeshift screen in his workshop, hiding from prying eyes.

But not Ian's. Ian could stand staring at that neglected but beautiful machine for hours on end, trying to figure out just where and how to start the daunting, but exciting task of getting the Jaguar to roar again.

Ian was under its spell. Benign or cursed? Or both? But once the euphoria had subsided and the practicalities of the task before him sank in, then the first worm of doubt, the first tremors of anxiety stirred in Ian Willard's breast.

Had he bitten off more than he could chew?

What did he really know about the intricacies of restoring an extremely valuable and rare vintage car? He had never moved in that rarified circle of obsessives and perfectionists who had spent a lifetime hunting down authentic parts, and who had an anecdote to tell about every wheel nut, every inner tube, every petrol cap they had traced to some unlikely source.

When Marcus had asked him if he should put the car in the hands of a vintage Jaguar specialist Ian had dismissed the idea. Why lose the potential profit to be made, yes, that was part of it, but how could he give up the once in a lifetime chance to fulfil an obsession?

As long as he could remember he had dreamed of discovering a truly classic vintage car. A 1930 four-and-a-half litre Bentley 'Blower'; a 1935 Bugatti 57SC Atlantic; a 1955 Mercedes Benz 300 SL Gull wing.

Or the 1938 Jaguar SS100 —and here it was in his workshop. Right here in his own workshop!

Before now Ian had 'restored' or done up old MGs, the occasional Lancia, early Ford Pilots, and had taken pride in the work, but if he couldn't find the exact part, the next best thing would do.

Not for this Jaguar it wouldn't. And that prompted another concern. Once he started to track down genuine parts for the SS 100 the enthusiasts would be alerted, and they wouldn't rest until they had hunted down the car in Ian's workshop. Perhaps with offers that could unsettle Marcus and their 'verbal' contract — which as Sam Goldwyn said —' is not worth the paper it's written on.'

And now the car was even more desirable than the moment Marcus had first pulled the dirty sheet from his 'old wreck'.

After they had struck a deal in Marcus' library, they had set out to explore the lofts above the garages, four in all, at the back of the Georgian mansion. Ian consumed with impatience, Marcus reluctant to leave the unconsumed wine.

It was clear that he was not a frequent visitor to his own garage lofts. It was Ian who had to find the light switches, before they climbed the rickety wooden stairs, clouds of dust meeting every footstep.

There was nothing to excite Ian in the first three, just some old and useless batteries, long empty oil cans, a few ancient car seats from undistinguished models, and rusty tools and, oddly, eight wheels, for a Ford Prefect.

Ian was hugely disappointed. He had hoped against hope that they might find at least some of the parts that were missing from the Jaguar in the stables.

They clambered into the final loft with little expectation.

The electric light did not extend to this last loft, and it took them a while to acclimatise to the pale shafts of light that filtered in from a small dirty window in the roof.

A hundred cobwebs clung to them as they made their way to a pile of what looked like parts in the corner, Marcus trying to pluck the silvery threads off his face and hair. 'God this is filthy,' he said with sour distaste.

But Ian wasn't listening. Ian had seen the wheels, with their seventy-two 18-inch spokes and the unmistakable SS insignia at the centre. Five of them, some sign of rust, the tyres flat, but otherwise in great condition. Oh my goodness.

Heart beating he pulled an old oily blanket from the rest of the pile and the large round headlamps, still with the original stone guards on them, stared proudly back as he stared round eyed at them.

'Marcus we need some more light, do you have a good torch in the house?'

'Must have. Yes we do.'

'Do you mind getting it?'

'What right now? What have you found?'

'Yes, if you don't mind.' Ian ignored the second question, and with some reluctance Marcus creaked back down the stairs.

An hour later they were sitting in Marcus' study poring over the papers that they had found in a small faded leather case also discovered under the blanket. To Marcus it was no more than a pile of old fading bills, to Ian it was a treasure chest.

'These bills are dated 1938. My God, this must be the original invoice from SS cars.

Look at this:- Jaguar SS 100, supplied to Sir Joseph Strickland, The Manor, Near Naunton, Cheltenham Gloucestershire........£445. Good lord. Well I suppose that was a tidy sum at the time. And here's a bill for some service from a local garage. 14 shillings and six pence.'

'But this is the real treasure - the log book. Just one owner, of course, your grandfather, stamped August 18th 1938, and the chassis number, the engine number, and the registered number plate - as on the car. This is such a bonus, Marcus.'

'Why's that old chap?'

'Why's that? Because it authenticates everything we could have wanted. This car is the real McCoy and here's the proof. There are any number of modern copies of the SS 100, now nobody can claim that this is one of them.'

'I don't see anyone mistaking *that* car for a modern copy.'

'Not now, I agree, but they might when we have finished restoring it. These papers are worth their weight in gold.'

'I see. So is the car more valuable than you thought? When you first saw it I mean? Now that we have found the wheels and the lights and these papers?'

'Yes it is, Marcus. I can't deny it. There is still an awful lot of work to be done on the car, but finding that hoard in your garage is certainly a step in the right direction.' He hesitated, Marcus was looking thoughtful. He decided. 'In fact, I think in the light of these 'finds' we should alter our deal, now, Marcus. You should take more of the profit?'

Marcus was gratified to hear these words, not for the money but for the confirmation that his friend was just as honest and fair as he believed.

'Oh dear, I'm hopeless at things like that,' he said, 'what do you suggest?'

'65% - 35%' a small voice of conscience whispered. Overruled.

'I think 55% to you and 45% to me.'

'Well, if you think so. But I don't want to do you down, old boy.' Marcus said.

Deborah had noticed the spring in Ian's step, the light in his eye, the moment he walked into the kitchen after his visit to see Marcus Strickland's old car.

'Well?' she asked.

'I've had a very interesting afternoon.'

She waited for him to go on, but he just smiled at her enigmatically.

'Why are you looking so smug?'

'Marcus' old wreck was a pre-war Jaguar.'

'A valuable pre-war Jaguar? By your 'cat's got the cream' smirk I should guess it probably was.'

'You know me too well, Mrs Willard. But yes, properly restored it would be valuable,' and he couldn't resist adding, 'very.' He saw the hope in Debbie's eyes. 'But at the moment it's in pretty bad shape.'

'And you'll restore it?'

'That's the idea.'

'And then Marcus will sell it?'

'No, we'll sell it. Marcus and I. We've done a deal. I'll do all the restoration, and we'll split the profit.'

'Is that fair to Marcus?' In just a few seconds his wife was pricking away at his conscience.

'The restoration will take months, if not years,' he pleaded his case, 'every washer, every cable, every stitch has to be authentic. If we can't find a part, we'll have to get it made, or make it. I'll be adding a hell of a lot of value.'

'Is it a fair deal for you, then?' Debbie didn't want her husband to lose out.

'Oh, I think so,' he said, but unfortunately he made it sound more like 'You bet it's fair to me!'

She studied him carefully. He was hiding something.

'What was the car, again?'

'A pre-war Jaguar.'

'I heard that. It's not like you to be so vague. What kind of pre-war Jaguar?'

'It's an SS 100, if that means anything to you. 1938.'

'So what would it be worth, all spruced up?'

'Quite a lot.'

'Ian. For goodness sake! £20,000? £50,000? More?'

'More. But before you get carried away, the restoration will cost a small fortune.'

But even as he said the words he knew that since they had uncovered that cache of missing parts in Marcus' loft, that the costs would be more small than fortune.

Now he suspected he might have to string out the restoration to reinforce his contribution to the project.

Ten days later the car was delivered to Willard's under cover of darkness, and for the next two weeks he took the first tentative and painstaking steps to remove the signs of neglect.

He washed the car first, with such careful concentration it took him two full days.

He gave it a first polish, cleaned the worst grime off the engine removed the mouse nest from the footwell, scrubbed up the wheels and just generally wandered around it in a state of awe.

Only then did Ian allow the frantically curious Debbie to come to the workshop and fall in love with it, as he knew she would.

'Oh, Ian, it's beautiful.'

The long louvered bonnet, and the large wire wheels, hastily put on so that the car could be pushed onto the transporter looked powerfully aggressive — but the flowing lines, the sweeping running boards, were silkily feline.

The grace of a prowling cat.

Ian's faithful old mechanics, George and Dave were proud as punch, too.

'Certainly is beautiful, Mrs. W.' She had never seen the usually dour George so animated, and she had never felt such excitement between these four walls. What a contrast to the stresses and worries of the last few months.

When Deborah returned home she did what Ian had guessed Marcus wouldn't do.

She made straight for her computer and in great excitement she Googled :- 'Jaguar SS100 1938'

She read the Wikipedia entry first, and then more and more of the 62,000 'hits' on the Google site.

And the more she read, the more uneasy she became. But why?

The eulogies for the car were unending. Not a single bad word about any aspect of the design, the engine, the performance. It was described as the very essence of the elegance and grace of the pre-war motor car.

Modern copies, 'nostalgia cars' they were called, were being snapped up in Britain and in America.

For about $100,000! For a copy.

As for the original models, well...Debbie was dumbstruck.

The very few that had been lovingly restored to their original condition were selling for staggering sums. £300,000, £415,000 and one sold at auction in America for £666, 270!

Deborah gazed at the screen in disbelief.

Did Marcus have any idea what his car could be worth? Would he ever have agreed to split the profit with Ian if he had known?

Of course not.

Maybe Ian, himself, she wondered, did not fully appreciate the fortune he could make from the sleek car in his workshop.

But of course he did. Even if he hadn't spent a lifetime drooling over vintage cars like the SS100, he would certainly have researched the going rate for one - just as she had.

He must have realised that the deal he had made with Marcus was grossly unfair to his friend. How could he have done it?

She knew, of course.

This incredible discovery was unbelievably timely. At a stroke, the profit from this one car would fund the Company's expansion plans, remove all the stress of that decision, and their perilous financial situation.

What a temptation it must have been, for her desperately worried husband. But how on earth could he have given in to it?

She didn't wait for Ian to come home. She didn't allow herself time to reflect. She raced straight back to the garage, barged into is office and tore into him before he could open his mouth.

'Ian I know what that car could be worth. I looked it up in Google. I couldn't believe my eyes. One was sold for well over half a million pounds —'

'That's nonsense.' Ian interrupted.

'—you can't possibly split the profits with Marcus. It's daylight robbery, it's probably criminal. You'll lose all credibility, not to mention all our friends, you've got to go and tell Marcus the truth, before he finds out for himself. I can't believe what you are doing Ian. You could still make a very decent profit even if Marcus takes the lion's share. Which you know he should. I can't believe what you are thinking of—'

'Calm down, Debbie.' He looked towards the door. 'And keep your voice down.'

'Why? Because you don't want George and Dave to know what a cheat their boss is?'

'No. Because you don't know what you are talking about.' He was getting angry, guiltily angry, perhaps, but he bridled at Debbie's unforgiving tone. What on earth did she know about it?

'Tell me then,' she challenged him.

'First of all, the car is in a very poor condition—"

'It doesn't look very poor to me.'

'It's been washed, for God's sake. Under the bonnet there's an engine that hasn't turned over for 50, 60 or maybe even 70 years. It will have seized up. The carpets and upholstery are mildewed, probably beyond repair, the glass in all the dials is foxed, and there's no gear handle, the tyres are perished, the power cables have perished but the generator may be saved. The carburettors and brakes will need weeks of painstaking attention, and may be too far gone. The electrics, the springs ... I could go on and on.'

'Twenty thousand pounds? Forty thousand pounds?'

'What are you talking about?'

'To restore the car. What will it cost?'

'It's impossible to tell.'

'Have a guess.'

DEBBIE, JUST SHUT UP!'

Even as he shouted the words Ian felt a surge of guilt. He and Deborah had never shouted at each other. Not once. But though he lowered it a little his voice lost none of its bitter hostility. 'Instead of charging in here, all steamed up because you've seen some silly prices on Google, you should be happy — for yourself, if you can't be happy for me. That car could be the saving of my business, and maybe even our house.'

'And what about Marcus? What will he get out of it, apart from a stab in the back?'

'You're very concerned about Marcus all of a sudden.'

'No, I am concerned about you, Ian.'

'Listen, for God's sake. Marcus had 'an old wreck' —that was his term for it, not mine — just sitting there and rusting away in his stables, taking up space. He would probably have paid me to take it away. If I had offered him £10,000 for it he would have bitten my hand off. But I didn't, I told him it was valuable—'

'Did you tell him how valuable?'

'—I told him it was valuable. I told him that if he let me restore it, and we split the profit he'd make a lot more than £10,000. And what's more when we found the wheels and the lights and the tonneau cover in his loft, I suggested he should get more than 50% and I should get less of any profit. He was a very happy man. He wants to see the car restored to its prime. I'll do that for him, and he'll make a very handsome profit. Not that he needs it, he's one of the richest men in the county. So don't worry too much about Marcus Strickland. Worry a bit more about Ian Willard.'

'I am worried about Ian Willard.'

'Hmmpf.'

'So what percentage of the profit will Marcus take now? 75%?' she nagged away at him. Wouldn't let it rest.

'Don't be absurd.'

'66%? 60%?'

'I am not prepared to discuss it.'

'No. I bet you're not. I wonder how many other secrets you have kept from me over the years?'

This was the cruellest cut of all. He and Deborah took the greatest pleasure in sharing all their thoughts, all their hopes , all their fears. How could she say such a thing? Hurt, alarmed, wracked with angry guilt, he lashed out.

'Damn you! Just go away and leave me to save our business and our house and our lives.'

She got up deliberately, walked over to him and slapped him hard across the cheek.

'I am glad your father can't see you now,' she said.

Stung by the slap, but stung so much more by her words, the unflattering comparison with his father, that he had spent so many years trying to convince himself was unjustified, he grabbed her roughly by the shoulders and pushed her violently towards the door.

"Just get out!'

How often would he replay that moment in his head. How often would he see his hands pushing roughly on her shoulders.

Propelled violently backwards, she tripped on an old leather case full of papers lying on the floor, and fell and hit her head with an awful thud against the corner of a steel filing cabinet.

She lay motionless. All her indignant energy of a few seconds ago, vanished. All his wrath turned to instant anguish.

He fell to his knees, and turned her head and saw the terrifying gash, the blood pouring from the wound, Debbie's face, ashen.

'GEORGE! DAVE!' He bellowed . 'QUICK! QUICK!'

They rushed in, they had been listening to the row from the office with growing disquiet. They had never heard Ian so angry. And with his adored Debbie, too.

'999, Ambulance. Hurry hurry, man,' Ian shouted desperately at George.

Tears were pouring from his eyes as he hopelessly tried to staunch the flow from the wound with his handkerchief, and George ran out to ring the emergency services.

George sat nervously on a plastic hospital chair as Ian paced up and down the corridor in barely controlled panic. 'Oh Debbie,' he kept muttering, 'Oh Debbie.'

'Can I get you some tea boss?' George had suggested once. 'Something stronger?'

But Ian saw and heard nothing.

'Oh Debbie.'

George's wife, Dot, had died in this hospital, five years earlier. It was the smell that brought it all back. That unmistakable anti-septic smell. And the echoes. Shoes clicking along unseen corridors, distant voices, sudden swishing activity as a nurse hurried by and was gone.

He wanted to leave, to go back to the house he now shared with his sister who had moved in to look after him when Dot died. And brought a husband. Peter. They didn't get on, George and Peter. They didn't fight, but they never went to the pub for a —

'Mr Willard?' George's aimless thoughts were interrupted by the young doctor's query.

'No.' He indicated Ian who was rushing towards them down the corridor.

Ian couldn't form the words. He couldn't ask. Without realising he had grabbed the young man's white coat and was staring wildly into his face.

The doctor gently removed Ian's hand.

'Let's sit down,' he suggested, and seeing Ian's look of panic added quickly 'I am very tired, I could do with a rest.'

Ian sat down, but shot up again at once.

'Your wife is still unconscious, but she has stabilised and her pulse and breathing are normal.'

'Oh thank God.'

'She has taken a very severe blow to the head, and is badly concussed. We cannot tell at this stage if there is any further damage. We'll have a better idea in the next few days, maybe even in the next 24 hours, when we hope your wife will regain consciousness. She's sleeping quite peacefully. Would you like to see her for a few minutes?'

Ian just nodded dumbly and followed the doctor along the corridor and through a door.

After five minutes George got up and went home.

Debbie did not regain consciousness in the next 24 hours, or in 'the next few days' as the doctor had suggested. She lay in a coma in Intensive Care for three weeks, hooked up to drips, watched over by screens that constantly monitored her heart, her Blood Pressure, her pulse, and watched over in despair by her husband.

In those three weeks Ian Willard lost two stone in weight and shed many litres of tears.

He sat by Debbie's bedside almost as immobile as she. He scarcely acknowledged the many visits that their friends made, and they left as concerned about him as they were about Debbie.

Later he wanted to thank those visitors for their kindness, but he just could not recall who they were.

When Helena arrived with Jasper from Scotland, and Bertram had flown in from Singapore, he had embraced his children with a fervour they had never before experienced. They tried to shake him from his anguish, to reassure him with their love, and Ian did appear to calm a little, but when they had gone he turned back to his wife lying so motionless beside him, and all his fears flooded through him once again.

It was as though he had caught his wife's coma —except that inside he was in turmoil. What had he done to his darling Debs! What had he done!

He had shouted at her. He had actually struck her. Pushed her violently, anyway.

And why? Because she had told him the truth. And he did not like that truth.

Those truths.

She had accused him of misleading, no, worse, of cheating, even defrauding Marcus Strickland. And he had. Perhaps not as badly as she had made it sound - he wasn't convinced that the car could possibly be worth the sums she had seen on the internet, even when perfectly restored. Could it? But all along hadn't he deliberately hidden from Marcus the value of his Jaguar? Yes he had.

And, worse, she had implied that he was not as good as his father - neither as a business man nor as a man.

'I'm glad your father can't see you now.' They were the last words Debbie had said to him. Would those awful words be the last he would ever hear from her lips?

All his life he had been compared to his father , or so he imagined, but refused to admit that he would never run the business as well, or never enjoy the respect of the community. Or the affection.

Praise heaped on his Dad's memory, 'Your old man was a one-off, Ian, a one-off.' filled him not with pride but with envy.

And now Debbie had uncapped the gusher, and he couldn't stop the truth welling up and bursting into his consciousness.

He was a failure. He had taken over a thriving business and turned it into a flop.

Debbie must have thought that all along, but for all their closeness, all the shared hopes and feelings, she had never once mentioned it.

She was too good for him.

That was another truth.

Sitting there by her hospital bed he spared himself nothing. He was a fool to think he could revive his failing garage by taking on BP. He hadn't got the nous.

He was a cheat. A swindler.

And a husband who didn't deserve the love of a wife he had nearly killed.

Why wouldn't she open her eyes and recognise him, oh how he wanted to pour out his heart to her.

The senior consultant, with the young doctor tucked in behind him, told Ian that these things take time, that they had hoped Debbie would regain consciousness sooner, but it was not unusual for the process to take as long as it was. But they talked seriously together in hushed tones that Ian couldn't hear.

Ian had fallen into a disturbed sleep in his chair by the bedside. His vigil was taking a heavy toll.

He was woken by a voice, and he looked round expecting to see the nurse.

The room was empty. He was dreaming.

'Ian?' faltering, sleepy.

He was at her side in an instant, looking down earnestly at her weakly flickering eyes.

'Debbie? Yes, It's Ian. Can you hear me?'

But she seemed to have slipped away again into unconsciousness.

Should he stay by her side, should he rush for a doctor. 'Nurse' he called quietly, he mustn't frighten Debbie, and no one answered his call.

Then he did run out and call the nurse.

'She called my name,' he told her. 'She said 'Ian'. It woke me.'

The nurse seemed unimpressed. She had watched this man deteriorate for the last three weeks. He might well hear voices in his fevered state. She resented his continual, mute presence, day after day. Getting under her feet.

She checked the monitors, wrote some notes on her chart and started for the door,

'Where am I?'

Ian Willard stared down at the car that had eaten so deeply into his thoughts while he had sat by Debbie's bedside. Gone was the euphoria. Gone was the excitement.

And soon gone would be the car itself. But the regret would linger long, long after.

My God she was a beauty. He ran his hand over the long bonnet, and sighed.

Finally 'This won't do,' he said aloud, 'let's get it over with.'

He picked up his car keys and left the workshop.

Marcus Strickland was taken aback to see Ian Willard standing on his doorstep.

Everyone knew that he was in a state of total shock after Deborah's accident. For three weeks they had talked of little else.

'Ian, old boy!' The gaunt face, the troubled eyes, the man looked terrible. 'Are you alright?'

'We need to talk.'

Marcus led him into the drawing room and they sat in deep armchairs either side of the beautifully carved Queen Anne fireplace, the hearth filled with summer flowers.

'How is Deborah? We were all so worried. And so pleased to hear that she is...awake, again.' Why was his friend, and now his partner, here looking so grim, so obviously ill at ease. It must be something to do with the Jaguar. Had he come to say that he couldn't do the restoration, now that his wife needed his care?

'Deborah is very weak. But she is sitting up in bed and talking, and eating a little real food. But she is very confused. She cannot remember anything about the accident, or much before it.' He sighed. 'She forgets words, places, things and people's names. The doctor's say it will take time, but they hope she will make good progress.' Ian spoke these words gazing towards the flowers in the hearth, but seeing only his wife in the hospital bed.

I am very happy to hear it.' Marcus said, unsure if Ian even heard him.

'They are giving her tests to do. Little children's puzzles. Jigsaws for two year olds.'

With an effort he pulled himself back to Marcus's house and Marcus, himself.

'Marcus I wish I had never set eyes on your bloody 'old wreck'. If Debbie doesn't ...' he faltered... 'if Debbie doesn't....' a long pause... 'I'll curse that car for ever more.'

'Steady on, old boy.' There was something in Ian's tone that suggested he'd curse Marcus for ever more as well. That was a bit thick. And anyway what had the car got to do with Deborah Willard cracking her head open on a steel cabinet. Ian was not making sense. 'What has my Jaguar got to do with it?'

Ian got up and walked to the window and looked out over the Park.

'Everything, Marcus, everything.'

'Go on.'

Then Ian turned and went back to his chair and said to Marcus the words that he had rehearsed so many times in his head in the past weeks.

He told him how his business was in trouble and about his plans— his expensive plans — to try and save it. How the car in Marcus' stable had appeared, like a gift from the gods, an answer to all his problems.

Then he told Marcus the difficult part, and maybe he wasn't totally honest even then. He said that from the moment he saw the car he knew it was worth a small fortune. Perhaps he had not given Marcus that impression, and he was ashamed that he had not been more open. But to be fair, he had not known the cost of restoring the car, and he had not quite realised what the car would be worth restored.

It was Debbie who had searched the internet and dug out some astonishing figures.

'What kind of figures?' Marcus wanted to know.

'£300,000. £350,000. Perhaps even more for such a well preserved model.'

There he had said it, and to his surprise, Marcus barely reacted.

'Hmm. A lot of money. Perhaps our 'deal' was not a very fair deal for me? What do you think Ian Willard?'

'No. it wasn't. It was ...despicably unfair.'

'Well, at least that's honest. Even if the deal wasn't.'

Neither spoke for some time.

'For what it's worth, and I don't see why you should believe me,' Ian said, 'but if the car *had* sold for that kind of money, I would have insisted you took the lion's share. I think I said something to that effect at the time.'

'No, I don't see why I should believe you, either.'

'I have not been fair to you, and I am very upset and sorry about it, Marcus.'

'And you'd like me to forgive you? Is that it, old boy'

Ian shrugged. 'I just wanted you to understand what I had done, and why. And to make amends, if I can.'

'Go on.'

'I will help you to find the right people to restore your car, and I will make sure that they offer you the very best deal. They will probably want to buy the car outright. I will negotiate the best possible price. I'll do everything I can to see you don't lose out.'

'You have lost interest in restoring it yourself, then?'

'I have, yes.'

He didn't say why and Marcus, curious as he was, didn't ask.

'But what about your plans to expand the business?'

'I have abandoned them.'

'You'll carry on as you are?'

'No. I shall try and sell the business - lock, stock and barrel.'

Marcus looked at his friend. All the stuffing had been knocked out of him, he could see that.

'You've had a bad time, old boy. Maybe, you should take it easy for a bit, before you make any big decisions. Think things over.'

'I have. Marcus I must go back to the hospital.' He rose and started to the door,

'I will contact some vintage car specialists in the next few days. I think you'll find that the local press and TV, and probably the national media, too, will be interested in the car once they hear what it could be worth. I've already had Autocar and Classic Cars onto me. God knows how they heard about it.'

'Oh Lord, I don't think I could handle that.' Marcus hesitated 'Ian I'd like to pass the media on to you. Can I do that, old boy?'

Ian's heart sank. he wanted nothing to do with 'that bloody car', but how could he refuse.

'Yes you can. But I won't have the car, that's what they'll want to film.'

Marcus followed Ian to the door 'You know, Ian, I am still quite happy for you to restore the car, and take a share — a smaller share — of the profits.'

Then Ian turned and looked properly at his friend for the first time. He squeezed Marcus' arm, tears jumping into his eyes.

Marcus felt both awkward and pleased at this simple gesture.

'Thank you Marcus. That's kind. And generous. But I shan't change my mind. Goodbye.'

'Goodbye, old boy.'

GRETA AS IN 'NOT BETTER'

Greta Davies is lonely.

The vivacious Swede sits in the cottage she bought with such delight and fashioned with such affection and pines for a partner to share it. Where is the vivacity, now? And the mirror, mirror on the wall reveals the first grey hairs among the sunshine blonde and what are euphemistically called 'laugh lines' around her eyes.

'Ha, ha, bloody-ha lines,' she calls them.

Those who sparkle in company feel the lack of it most keenly. You will never hear Greta Davies complain, ' I want to be a-l-o-o-n-e', like her legendary namesake Greta Garbo.

It is scant consolation to know that men find her desirable, when those same suggestive flirts dine happily with their families, while she heats her Waitrose dinner-for-one.

But, of course, she is not always alone.

She is not alone in the travel agency, and to the frustration of her two young assistants — neither long married — seems reluctant to shut up shop and release them to their partners.

And she has a social life — of sorts.

She is invited to parties but less frequently to dinners, where the middle England compulsion to have balanced numbers of hims and hers weighs against her, or at best pairs her with a sad widower, or a man whose inclinations make him impervious to her charms.

And she does join in; pilates once a week; the book group once a month; and a visit from her mother once a year, which she invariably looks forward to with pleasure and back on with irritation.

There's the cinema society, the rambling group and the tennis club which she joined in a rush of New Year enthusiasm, but on reflection, and fearful of improbable humiliations on court, has never visited.

But there are many times when Greta sits alone, and feels all too far from her homeland. She aches for the chaos, the laughter, the love of the boisterous log cabin farmhouse of her childhood. The sunny, splashing, screeching, summers; the peace of the snow muffled winters around the comforting tiled stove.

She would like to meet a man.

An interesting and interested man.

A kind and funny and thoughtful — but purposeful — man.

Above all, an unattached man.

Such a paragon is not easily run to ground in London let alone Cheltenham.

And in Greta's sleepy Cotswold village?

Just once, perhaps.

One warm summer evening a most beautiful young man cruised into the village in his scarlet Ferrari 458 Italia Spider and stopped outside The Black Horse Inn. He sat at one of the tables in the garden an iced lemonade holding down one corner of a map that he was studying intently.

And in no time the manager of the Inn, two barmaids, three locals at nearby tables, and a woman walking her dog were gathered round the map anxious to help a stranger to the village. (The village attracted many strangers — but few were showered with such solicitude.)

Had they a room, he asked, for a day or two? He was charmed by the Inn, the village and the area, he said to his admiring audience.

And the Inn, the village and the area were certainly charmed by him.

The men drawn to his easy manner, engaging smile, and flattering interest in their lives; their wives and girlfriends beguiled by the unwavering confidence in those deep blue eyes. Indeed, they found it hard to look at anything else if he was within smiling distance. Curiosity in the village was near fever pitch.

But when he and his scarlet Ferrari 458 Italia Spider purred out of their lives five days later they knew no more about him than the moment he drove into them.

He left behind nothing but a worried barmaid and a name —James Penney — and even that doubtful, for their eager Google searches found no celebrity, no film star, no multi-millionaire of that name.

Perhaps, after all, their perfect man was just a mirage.

But Greta, visiting a distant cousin in distant Copenhagen, missed this improbable chance. And just as well.

She does have every reason to be wary of Englishmen.

First Peter Davies so devoted and charming in Sweden, so devious and cruel in Swindon. Her miserable twelve month marriage in that grim basement flat had done nothing to endear her to the men of her adopted country.

She had been pawed by the plumber, and groped by Derek Henderson and, far more seriously, assaulted by a client in Gloucester.

The rough, gross Mr Henry Chapple, owner of Chapple Haulage, was considering a four week cruise for himself, his wife and his three fat children.

'Nothing but the best, love. First class suites, the whole bloody caboodle,' he had insisted to Greta.

You bent over backwards to keep such clients happy — but not literally. Mr Chapple thought otherwise. He invited Greta to bring details of the trip to his vulgar new house in Painswick, and there attempted to rape her.

She arrived to find him there alone, and without any preamble he flung her holiday itinerary onto an erotic Allen Jones coffee table, and then flung himself onto Greta.

In fear and desperation she fought as best she could, but he was heavy and strong and forced her down onto the floor, and tore at her clothes.

Only the crunch of tyres on gravel, the sudden sweep of headlights across the room, the pathetic panic of the mighty haulage tycoon saved her.

Greta, sobbing, clothes torn, cheek bruised fled from the house as the 'not expected' wife approached the front door.

Greta won't easily forget the look on Mrs Chapple's face. It registered no shock, no sympathy not even anger. Only contempt. Sneering contempt for Greta. Well hidden contempt for her hectoring husband. And maybe contempt for her timid, subservient self.

The police were sympathetic, but Henry Chapple was a man of influence, and after one brief interview with him, but not Mrs Chapple who had left hastily for their villa in Marbella, and a note from the Deputy Chief Constable, they were 'persuaded' that there was insufficient evidence against Henry Chapple to prosecute the case any further.

And Greta Davies became just one more foreigner disillusioned with the much vaunted British sense of Justice.

After that Greta looked overseas, and discovered a Scandinavian dating agency for ex-patriots in Britain. But that was little better.

She endured a tedious dinner with the dreariest of Danes in Oxford; and a much more exciting weekend with a charming Swede in a smart hotel in The Cotswolds. But her high hopes of him were dashed when three days later the not-so-charming-after-all Swede, rang from Los Angeles. He had neglected to tell Greta that he lived in America with a wife and two small boys — but didn't see them as any impediment to him meeting up with her on his business trips to England. She was very gratified that she could vent the full range of her contempt for him and his suggestion in her native tongue.

Greta did lose heart after that.

And then — Marcia Woodrow.

After their lunch in Winchcombe which had led to that afternoon of such unguarded passion, Greta had wondered if she might repeat the invitation, or even wanted to.

She understood that for Marcia it was a one-off experiment — one that she had conducted with enthusiasm, certainly — but was unlikely to repeat.

Marcia had not tried to avoid Greta since that day, but nor had she given the least acknowledgment of any shared and secret intimacy.

It was as though she had airbrushed it out of her memory as effectively as her husband airbrushed the blemishes out of an advertising photograph.

Which only added to Greta's loneliness. She badly missed the closeness she had felt for those few brief hours. Not the physical closeness, either.

For the first time in her life she had felt that she had found another human being to whom she could be utterly honest — more honest, perhaps than she could be even with herself.

'But the fucking fucking has fucked up the chance,' she said aloud bitterly; demonstrating a sure command of the coarser use of the English language.

On the other hand how long would it have taken to have forged such closeness without the fucking fucking?

Oh, it was all so complicated.

Greta had not met Marcia alone, since 'the lunch'.

She had walked past Marcia's gallery in Cheltenham, many times, without finding the courage to enter, and she scolded herself for her cowardice.

What could be more natural than popping in to see her friend? And what was the worst that could happen?

And then one day she did pluck up the courage.

Marcia Woodrow's gallery on the Promenade in Cheltenham was a surprising success. Well, it surprised Marcia, if not Brian who recognised his wife's eye for the more moving and accomplished art.

And soon she was displaying a flair for publicity, a very good head for business and a keen eye for a bargain, as well.

The Gallery was not large, but it was superbly located and Marcia had none of the haughty airs that gallery owners so often assume to justify their superior prices.

The soft colours and the pretty flowers, the ever open door made 'Fine Pictures' an easy place to browse. And once lured in you found yourself persuaded in the gentlest possible way, that the picture which had caught your eye in the window, had always been destined to hang above your fireplace.

This was the gallery that Greta Davies walked into one bright spring morning in May. She had rehearsed in her head, over and over, what she would say, but, alas, there was no Marcia to say it to.

'Can I help you?'

Paula Duncan, Marcia's bright young assistant, gave the warm, welcoming smile her employer insisted on.

'Oh, er no. I was just looking...' she hesitated.

'Oh yes, please look around, and do tell me if you need any help.'

'No, I was just looking for Marcia, actually.'

'Mrs Woodrow is on the 'phone at the moment.'

And, indeed, Greta could hear Marcia talking in the office at the rear of the gallery.

'Oh. Perhaps I better come back another time.'

'She won't be long, I think.'

And then Marcia appeared and smiled warmly, but whether it was professional or personal Greta couldn't tell.

'Hello Greta. Have you come to buy a picture?'

Greta looked around vaguely at the paintings. 'Not really,' she said.

Marcia glanced briefly at Paula.

'Come through into the office.'

The office door had barely closed behind them before Greta was blurting out the suggestion of lunch sometime . 'Nothing fancy. Just a salad, round the corner.'

Marcia hesitated. 'Well, I'm not sure if —'

'Not like...well you know…last time,' Greta jumped in, 'I just wanted to talk.'

Marcia studied Greta for a few seconds, wondering if she would be tempted again by the sensual Swede. No, not for a moment, she realised. Their afternoon in Greta's bed had been cathartic. But final.

'Alright, Greta,' she said, 'what about today?'

And that's how Greta and Marcia became close friends again. Nothing physical, of course. That was firmly agreed by both within minutes of sitting down for their simple lunch in a crowded cafe. No uneaten Foie Gras and Sea Bass this time. And certainly no afters.

Greta, as always, was very direct and open, and Marcia wondered if such openness made her vulnerable. Did men see it as an invitation? From what Greta told her that day it seemed they did. Peter Davies, the plumber, Derek Henderson, the ghastly Henry Chapple, it all came tumbling out. My God, had the indiscreet Greta told anyone — everyone — about their uninhibited afternoon? She doubted it but she did ask.

'Oh Marcia! How could you think that!' The hurt in Greta's eyes was all the persuading Marcia needed.

No, Greta confided, she would never tell a living soul. But apart from the — well, what they had agreed would never be repeated — she had felt a wonderful connection with Marcia; an overwhelming closeness. She had felt they could say anything, share anything. And she missed that very much. Would Marcia please be her special friend, she pleaded. She told Marcia that she was often very lonely in her cottage, and how lovely it would be if she, Marcia, could come and share it with her now and again. Just to talk, she added quickly.

Marcia listened intently, searching for something unsaid. She couldn't find it.

'Yes, Greta. Let's be friends.'

'Special friends?' She could have been thirteen, smoking behind the bike shed.

'Good friends,' Marcia conceded. 'And I am sorry you're lonely, Greta. When you have family, you forget how lonely people can be without one. We must have you round more often. I am sure Brian won't mind... I think he is a little smitten with you.'

'I've asked Greta Davies round to supper on Wednesday, Brian. Will you be here?'

Brian looked up sharply from his Sudoku. 'Why not? I usually am. Do you want me to go out? Is that what you're saying?'

'Don't be silly. Of course I don't. She came into the gallery the other day, and we had lunch. She gets very lonely in her cottage, she told me. I thought we should have her around more often, that's all.'

Brian watched her over his paper, as she bustled around the kitchen. He had not forgotten, of course, Julia's nasty innuendo on his tape recording. But since that day he had not noticed the least difference in his wife, nor had he heard another shred of rumour about her and Greta.

And anyway hadn't he actually suggested something about Greta Davies sharing their marital bed? What had he been thinking of?

So Brian was quite satisfied that Julia Strickland was not just a compulsive talker, but a compulsive trouble-maker, as well. At the lunch when she had revealed her 'news' about Marcia and Greta, she had been edged out of the conversation, and no doubt would have said almost anything to attract attention.

But now here was Marcia suggesting they — or did she mean she — should welcome Greta into their home, more often. Had Julia been right after all?

It was a situation ripe for suspicion, misunderstanding and recrimination.

They couldn't easily discuss it, for both had a secret best kept to themselves.

Marcia was determined that not a hint of her brief liaison with Greta should ever reach Brian's ears. She would never mention it, and nor would Greta, she was sure.

And Brian could not air his misgivings without revealing the source of them — that damned tape recording.

So when Marcia innocently prattled on about Greta he must keep his mouth shut, but his eyes wide open.

He was brooding on these matters when the telephone rang.

Greta? he wondered.

Marcia picked up the phone, spoke briefly and brought it over.

'It's Derek,' she mouthed.

Derek Desmond was Brian's Director of design, and right hand man. They often talked over problems in the evening, to both Marcia's and Judith Desmond's disapproval. Wasn't that what the office was for?

Brian took the phone.

'Yup?' he said.

Derek Henderson was taken back by such a curt, dismissive greeting. Was it that damned letter of his? Was he losing the respect of his friends?

'Hello Brian. It's Derek Henderson. You sound...preoccupied.'

'No, no. Not at all. I thought it was Derek from the office. We're not very formal on the telephone.'

'Oh.' Derek was reassured. Not the 'letter' after all. 'Have you got a moment, I have something I'd like to discuss with you.'

'Sure.'

'It's about Jim Ward. It's a bit... delicate.'

'OK. But you do know Jim and Vivienne are friends of ours, Derek?'

'I know that. He's a friend of mine, too. And I hope that anything I say about Jim won't go any further.'

Brian just said, 'Go on.'

'Well it's about Jim's driving ban. I agreed to act as guarantor for his fine, with the Court.'

'I see. £1,500, wasn't it? He hasn't stopped complaining about it.'

'I know. I know. But twice the legal limit at six o'clock in the evening, what did he expect?'

Brian didn't respond and Derek ploughed on, 'Anyway, he wrote a cheque for £500 in the court which would have bounced.'

'Ah.'

'I had to give him the money to cover it. Since then another payment, also for £500, became due and he wrote another cheque which would have bounced.'

'Ah, again.'

'So, again, I gave him the money to cover it, as his guarantor I had no option. In two weeks time...well you get the gist.'

'I do. But I can't see why you're telling me all this?'

'Well, in a nutshell, Jim tells me that he will be able to repay the money quite soon — because he is expecting a commission from you. Quite a large job, apparently.'

'I see.' Brian was wondering how much he should divulge to Derek Henderson.

It wasn't really any of his business.

Brian Woodrow had given freelance work to Jim Ward for some years, and was generally pleased with the result.

But for a while now Jim had become increasingly unreliable. His work always had arrived late but now it was second rate, as well. Brian could tell at a glance that it had been dashed off at the last minute.

Then one day Jim arrived for a meeting with a client at Woodrow Design late and drunk. He had insulted the client, the client's product, and even the client's wife.

It had cost Brian a day at Cheltenham Races, followed by dinner at The Champignon Sauvage, to mollify Mr and Mrs client. And there would be no more work for Jim Ward. Friend or no.

So what should he tell Derek Henderson?

'I was just wondering if that was the case,' Derek continued, when Brian didn't answer. 'Whether I could stop hounding him for the money? Maybe I shouldn't ask you, Brian. But it would make it easier if I knew.'

'Yes, well. I don't know what to say, Derek. Or rather, I don't know how much I should say. As you know I have used Jim to do work for me, in the past—'

'Yes. He tells me, in fact I think he tells everyone, that you like his work. Sorry, I interrupted.'

'And, yes, on the whole, I've been pretty happy with it.'

'But?'

'But I have no immediate plans of using him, again.'

'No big contract, then?'

'No big contract.'

Derek sighed 'Well, I can't pretend to be very surprised. Poor Jim. He's his own worst enemy. Well thanks for telling me Brian. It's not very reassuring, but it's good to know.'

'No problem. But I'm sure you won't pass on that information to Jim.'

'Don't worry, I won't, even if he brings up the 'big job' you're going to give him.'

'I think that would be best.'

'Looks like I've been hoist by my own petard. I talked up his fine, and now I'm the one who's paying it. Ironic, really. Anyway, how are you coping with this recession, Brian? Isn't advertising one of the first businesses to suffer?'

'We're doing OK. Revenue is down slightly, but we've cut costs accordingly. The legal profession is no doubt booming?'

'Not bad. When the going gets tough, the tough get going to their lawyers...so they say. Bankruptcies, repossessions, disputes...'

'It's an ill wind.'

'Exactly. But I could still find time for a game of golf, if you're interested.'

'Sure, maybe in a couple of weeks.'

'I'll give you a ring. And thanks again for the Jim thing.'

He had hardly put the phone down, when Marcia mentioned Greta again.

'I thought when Greta came to supper on Wednesday we could have Jim and Viv over as well.'

'Oh dear. You haven't asked them yet, have you?'

'Well, sort of, yes. I met Viv in Tesco's and mentioned it. Why 'Oh Dear'?'

'It appears Derek's paying Jim's drink-driving fine, and can't get the money back. But Jim's told him that he's getting a big freelance job from me.'

'And he isn't?'

'No. And not likely to in the future. Big or small.'

'I thought you liked his work, Jim always says you do.'

'So it seems. And I did. But it's really sloppy now. He's a boozer, and it's showing in his work. He rang last week and asked about any jobs that might be coming his way. I thought it best to level with him.'

'I see. What did he say?'

'Not much. He called me a fucking cunt and slammed the phone down. He sounded pissed.'

'How unpleasant. Well I better ring Viv and make some excuse about supper on Wednesday.'

'Such as?'

'I'll think of something. I'll probably blame you.'

Brian laughed. He guessed she probably would.

After a while she said, almost to herself 'I wonder if I should invite Horace Eastham on Wednesday?'

She would never cease to surprise him.

'Horace Eastham! Horace Eastham? The man who never speaks, the man with the list of questions? A man who never accepts an invitation? Not that he gets them anymore. What an extraordinary idea.'

'I know, I know it sounds loopy. But didn't you see Horace and Greta at the Stricklands' party? They were getting on like a house on fire.'

'Can't say I noticed.'

'Well everybody else did. They were talking together for hours. And Horace was talking more than she was.'

'Well he won't come, anyway.'

'He might if he knows Greta is coming. It's just a harmless bit of matchmaking.'

'Horace? No chance. He won't come, anyway,' he repeated, as though that settled the matter.

But Horace did come. And, as Marcia suspected, Greta had been the lure.

It had been an awkward telephone call. In the first place Horace clearly had great difficulty in placing Brian and Marcia.

'Did they have any children at Pate's?' He'd asked, hoping to fix the parents through the pupil. Marcia explained they had no children, and then, as casually as she could, asked Horace if he was free to come to supper on the following Wednesday.

Horace, his alarm clearly audible, had declined the invitation almost before it had left her lips.

Marcia said that she was sorry that Horace would not be able to come as she had invited Greta Davies, and she had hoped that Horace could make up the numbers. Horace had been silent for so long that Marcia had supposed he had rung off, but just as she was about to replace the receiver, Horace had said that actually he found he was free on that night, and that he would be happy to accept their invitation. He then asked, yet again, who had invited him, and where they lived and what date and time the dinner was.

When Marcia put the 'phone down she glanced across to Brian, who gave no impression that he had been listening to Marcia's call, but clearly had, and told him that Horace was, indeed, coming on the following Wednesday.

'I hope you don't regret it,' he said.

Marcia went to her gallery on the following Wednesday, but surprised Paula Duncan by leaving at lunch time. Paula had never before had the responsibility for the gallery for so long. She swelled with pride. She would have given her right arm to have sold a picture that afternoon, but fortunately she didn't and so was able to keep her unoffending limb.

The supper party — or rather, the supper, as any sense of a party was conspicuously absent — was a very strange affair, indeed. In view of their histories together, perhaps it was not altogether surprising.

There was Marcia, determined to put her intimacy with

Greta firmly behind her, and encourage the Swedish beauty to transfer it to Horace Eastham.

There was Brian, who having persuaded himself that Julia Strickland's taped insinuations about Greta and his wife were groundless, was now on the alert, looking for the least sign that they weren't.

There were two Gretas.

The Greta who was anxious to be as charming as possible to Marcia in order to cement their new friendship, and so unwittingly to rouse Brian's suspicions.

And the Greta who was acutely embarrassed to find that Horace — the poor man that she had led on and then rejected — was also present. What would he do, what would he say? She hardly dared look at him, lest, thus encouraged, he launched into another declaration.

And there was Horace. He had come hoping that his invitation had been at Greta's suggestion, and perhaps to rekindle the closeness he and she had experienced at the Stricklands' party. But how could he do so with these two strangers present?

He had already forgotten their names. He sat there tongue-tied, and losing confidence by the minute.

Oh, why hadn't he bought his list of questions!

Marcia did her best.

She asked Horace about his teaching, she asked him about his flat above the Stricklands' stables, his holidays, his interests; and to every question she received so short and final an answer, all addressed towards Greta, that she ran out of topics even before they sat down to eat.

During the meal Greta and Marcia kept up a desperate dialogue to fill the awkward silences, while the two men sat and studied Greta.

Horace to find any sign of encouragement for himself, and Brian to find any sign of a special intimacy with his wife.

Neither could feel satisfied by the scrutiny. Both felt that Greta spent far too much energy, too much vivacity, relating to Marcia.

At last it was over. And thank the Lord for that, thought Marcia. What a mistake to ask the painfully non-committal Horace. And how wrong she had been about him and Greta. They hardly exchanged two words. And Brian hadn't helped — he had just sat there brooding. Why on earth had he been so taciturn? The whole evening had been an unmitigated disaster.

It came, therefore, as a huge surprise to Marcia when Greta, as a 'special friend', had confided in her a few weeks later that she and Horace were seeing each other on a regular basis.

'Goodness me, Greta, I'm dumbstruck! How? Why?'

Then, as usual with Greta, it all came out in a rush. How she had deliberately set out to attract Horace at the Stricklands' party, and how she had done it far too well. The tea and buns in Cheltenham where she had firmly closed the door on his hopes. Her embarrassment when she had found Horace at the supper.

'So what on earth's happened since?' Marcia's eyes shone with curiosity.

'Well, Horace left your house some time before me that night, and as I drove home I saw him striding along the lane ahead of me. It was a miserable wet night so I offered him a lift. I wouldn't have stopped if it had been dry.'

'But you did. And then what?'

'He was...well, different, somehow. He didn't pour out his heart as he had before. In fact he said very little. And when we got to his flat he just thanked me for the lift and got out of the car. I lowered the window and asked him if he was alright. I don't know why. He leaned towards the window; the rain was drumming on the roof of the car, I remember…streaming down his face like tears.

He said he was sorry for the way he had behaved before, that he shouldn't have said what he did, even if he meant it. He said he might be very clever — I'd told him how clever he was at the Stricklands' party when I was 'chatted him up', is that the English expression? — but he wasn't clever enough to know, he said, how to behave to such a nice lady as me. Nice. Not beautiful, not attractive, not stunning — all the usual male flattery. But nice. I really liked that. I told him he was much nicer than me, and I meant it. I told him to go inside, he was getting soaked. But he just stood there, and then he asked me if I would consider having tea and buns with him again in the same funny cafe. And I said yes.'

This time Horace had arrived at the cafe only five minutes early, and Greta was already there. Patty Wenman, the pretty young waitress that Horace had taught at Pate's had left with Raleigh International for Nicaragua, and an older, bored waitress shuffled over to take their orders. The buns were no fresher than on their first visit.

But the great difference was to be found either side of their small, rickety table.

Horace had lost most of his desperation, and Greta most of her impatience.

They talked of this and that and even about the weather — imagine, Horace Eastham talking about the weather — before finally they eased into talking about themselves.

The tongue-tied Horace, and the recklessly ardent Horace were replaced by a thoughtful (no doubt a deeply thoughtful)

Horace. And the flirtatious Greta, and the judgemental Greta, were replaced by a gentler Greta. A woman of 39 who was lonely and grateful for the much more careful affection that Horace now expressed towards her.

It was a cautious first step. Both were anxious not to rush. Like a couple walking arm in arm on an icy path, both would fall if either slipped. And they did look a very strange match; the lanky English eccentric and the lovely Scandinavian. But when they left the cafe a full two hours later, neither doubted that the first step would be followed by others.

And it is pleasing to report that neither was unhappy at the prospect.

Marcia reported the surprising news to Brian with glee.

'Guess who our voluptuous Greta is 'walking out with', Brian?'

For a split second he froze. But, no, Marcia was far too relaxed to make any alarming announcements.

'Walking out with? How very Victorian. Who?'

'Guess. And a clue — I played Emma.'

The BBC had just serialised the Austen novel, so Brian understood the reference to the meddling matchmaker.

'Horace Eastham,' he said, laughing, thus unwittingly spoiling her great revelation.

'Yes. Horace Eastham.'

Brian remembered the painful supper the four had shared.

'Impossible,' he said.

Then Marcia recounted her conversation with Greta with such pleasure that if Brian did have any lingering doubts about Julia Strickland's innuendos on the tape, they were buried there and then.

So he listened with great satisfaction to Marcia's story. But his sense of relief was tempered with a sense of his own stupidity.

It was he, in that noisy steak restaurant in Las Vegas, who had set the hare running in the first place.

Too much steak. That's what he'd said. Too much steak would be boring.

Thank God Marcia hadn't listened to him.

A small celebration might be in order he thinks.

'I think I might open a bottle of the '98 Lynch Bages, darling, can I tempt you?'

'OK, why not. But just a glass.'

Thanks

To all those who bullied me first to write and then to publish these stories — a big thank you.

Particularly, Jeremy Barlow, John Gordon, Simon Lister, David Kaye, Oliver (and Sue) Gillie, Margaret Evison, George Krugier, Nick Merriman, Harry Rutherford, my reading group, the Calton Club, all those who I will remember the moment the book has gone to press. And even more particularly, my wife Ann.

I am grateful to Spiffing Covers, too, for their cheerful professionalism.

And if no-one buys these stories, well, I've got birthday and Christmas presents sorted for years to come.